Ends of the Earth

Naomi Starkey

MINSTREL
Eastbourne

First published 1992

Front cover by Rodney Matthews.

ISBN 0 85476 291 4

Minstrel is an imprint of Kingsway Publications Ltd,
1 St Anne's Road, Eastbourne, E Sussex BN21 3UN
Typeset by Nuprint Ltd, Harpenden, Herts
Printed in Great Britain by BPCC Hazells Ltd,
Aylesbury, Bucks.

Contents

PART ONE

'I sit at the bottom of these high walls
the baked walls of a city
watching the slow approach of a stranger
along the path through the dunes
along the path from the coast.'

From *Nineveh* by Mike Starkey.

1

The Pilgrim

I, Brendan, have decided to set down a full account of the matter. I was the one who heard the tale and my heart will not be eased until I have recorded it, as faithfully as I can.

Three summers ago, in the 546th year since the birth of our Lord, our brotherhood won permission from the abbot to build a community on the storm-battered western coast of Arainn, largest of the three islands which people call Ara na Naomh, Aran of the Saints, because of the many holy men who have prayed and studied and worshipped God here. Our community is nothing grander than a row of stone cells within a sheltering wall, where the twelve of us live and work together, seeking the voice of the Lord God in prayer and meditation. In gentle weather it is a pleasant place, when sunlight and shadows play over the grey rocks and the silence is broken only by the surf thundering against the cliffs and the seabirds' cries. When the winter gales begin, the icy rain and hail lash the ground and we huddle in the darkness, pleading for God's mercy and the coming of spring.

Our cliff top is too bleak for growing food, so we raise crops of oats and barley on a couple of fields inland where the air is kinder. The monks of Arainn are famed for their austere lives and as our founder Abbot Enda decreed, we do not eat meat or drink wine and at night we sleep on beds of stone, wrapped in our woollen habits.

Despite the cruel storms of our second winter, we managed to build ourselves a small oratory, a place where we could meet in worship. We have no reliquaries or jewelled chalices to make it beautiful, but we inlaid the walls with crosses of white quartz and the roof is snug and rainproof. Brecan, eldest of the brothers, told us that our Lord desires a pure mind and undivided heart rather than fine ornaments, so we are content.

Thus the history of our community, the home of the twelve brothers, perched on a windswept promontory which some say is the western edge of the world. Beyond our cells is nothing but the cliffs, and beyond them the grey ocean.

It was to this community, five days ago, that two women brought an old, old man who they said had come on a currach—a fishing boat—from the mainland, asking the way to the brothers in the West. Thinking he could only mean our community and seeing that he was too weak to walk up to the cliffs, the kindhearted women all but carried him here from their village and left him with pitying glances and smiles. Although we do not yet have a place to house pilgrims, not expecting anybody to journey to such a desolate spot, we found shelter for the traveller in an empty cell used for storing provisions in the winter months. As the youngest of our brotherhood, I was given the task of attending the old man and supplying his needs until he was strong enough to tell why he had journeyed to us.

Since our own beds were too hard for a sick man, we settled him on a makeshift couch of the sheepskins which we sometimes used on the coldest nights. When the other brothers returned to their cells for prayer, I went back to see the pilgrim, bringing him some newly-baked bread and a cup of water. He lay quite still, apparently asleep, with one thin hand resting on the heavy coverings spread over him. I had never before seen a man quite so old, his hair as white as sea-foam, his worn skin stretched tight over the cheekbones. The silvery lines of a scar ran like a cobweb from above his left eye, scoring deep across his cheek and down to the corner of his mouth, twisting and puckering the features so that from one side the face was grotesque. As I came closer for a better look at him, my shadow passed across his face and immediately he was awake, sunken eyes kindling like live coals. Such eyes! Not merely old but ancient, the eyes of one carrying a great weight of knowledge and experience and, surely, suffering.

Clumsy boy that I am, I blundered out the first words that came into my head. 'Who are you?'

A trace of a smile lingered on the old man's lips as he replied, 'No more than a pilgrim, my son. A tired old pilgrim longing for his final rest.'

'By what name shall we call you?'

The old man made a small gesture with his hand, dismissing a matter of no importance. 'Call me father, pilgrim, old fellow, what thou wilt. Names do not matter to me.'

I offered him the bread and water but he would only drink a little, saying he needed no food, only rest and quiet.

'Have you travelled far to come here, Father?' I asked as I straightened his coverings.

Again I saw a gleam of amusement on his face. 'If I told thee how far and how hard I have journeyed, my son, thou wouldst not believe me.' Something about his eyes made me hesitate to dismiss his words as boastful.

Wishing him a good night, I was about to leave when one of his wrinkled hands darted out and clutched the sleeve of my habit.

'Tell me, my son,' he whispered, so softly that I had to stoop to catch the words, 'are there any lands west of here?'

'None that I know of. Some people call this cliff top the westernmost edge of the world. You cannot go any further.'

'Ah!' He sighed a long, satisfied sigh and closed his eyes, relaxing his hold on my sleeve. Sleep took him even as I watched.

I rose early the next morning, while a clammy sea mist still cloaked the promontory. Although spring was in full bud in the lowland fields, the nights were still bitter up on the cliffs and I was concerned for the comfort of the old pilgrim.

When I entered the cell, he was lying as I had left him on the previous evening, flat on his back, hands smoothed over the covers, but his eyes were wide open and he turned as soon as I stepped over the threshold.

'You slept well, Father?' I asked politely. 'These spring nights are cold and I know Arainn can offer warmer places of rest than our cells.'

'I have slept well, my son. I have had beds far colder and harder than this.'

I could no longer contain my curiosity. 'Why have you come here, Father? All the holy places and shrines are on the eastern side of the island.' He stared back at me without replying until I blushed at my impertinence. 'Forgive me, Father, I did not mean...'

'No matter. Thou art a boy and boys are right to ask questions. I am, as I have said, a pilgrim, bound for the West. My path led me here and I hope that I have come to the end of my journeying at last.' I think he could read my thoughts which were bursting with questions, because he added, 'What more wouldst thou know?'

What more? In all my seventeen years I had only met a mainlander twice, and no one as strange as this old man. What could I say? Before I opened my mouth, he ran a finger down the silver lines of his scar. 'Maybe thou wouldst know how I came by this mark?' I blushed, for that was the very question I longed to ask. 'Do not worry. Thy curiosity is not wrong.' He looked past me to the open doorway where the sun was melting the mist. 'It is a very long tale and one which I have never cared to tell another soul. But perhaps this morning…' his eyes bore into me until I dropped my gaze to the ground. 'Perhaps I will tell it, if thou wilt listen. I think the right time has come.' He pointed to the end of the bed and, wonderingly, I took my seat there.

2

At the Beginning

Once there were four people—a family—living more years ago than anyone could count, in a far-off, empty land. It was a country of remote uplands and craggy mountains, and the family had made their home in one of the caves which honeycombed the lower hills, opening onto a little plateau where their flocks grazed. The cave sheltered them from the winter rains and the gusting winds of spring, and offered a cool refuge from the fierce heat in summertime.

The father and mother of the family had been grey-haired as long as their sons could remember and their faces were always weary. The father's back was stooped after a lifetime of labouring at the thin soil to grow crops and tending his sheep and goats. Care had etched deep lines on the mother's face. Although their lives had been nothing but toil from dawn till dusk for many seasons, their hearts were cheered by the sight of their two growing sons whose strong arms took charge of more and more of the work as time passed.

Although Hevel, the younger of the two, could run faster and throw a hunting spear further than his brother, he had always been slow in speech and thought. He took care of the family flocks under his brother's orders and liked nothing better than to roam the hills all day long, searching out the best grazing. From time to time he would shout just to hear the echo. What he shouted most often was his mother's name because he said he loved her more than anyone else in the world, and sometimes he shouted his brother's name because he also loved him very much.

Kayin, the elder, used his own quick wits and deft fingers to turn the empty little mountain plateau from a haphazard division of pasture and field into a garden. While his father used to raise his crops in cramped rows divided by paths of bare earth, Kayin spent hours planting the barley, lentils and wheat in green circles and spirals, and encouraged the fine upland grass to grow in between. After digging pools to store water from the winter rains, he channelled it into a network of streams and rivulets so that the sound of running water filled the garden, and in springtime the wild flowers sprang up from the damp earth like tiny jewels—scarlet, ivory, saffron, violet, crimson and midnight blue. Sometimes he would leave his work for a day and tramp the hills with his brother, searching for new plants. Sometimes Hevel would pen the flocks in a cave and wander down to the wide plains beyond the hills, returning late in the evening with a clutch of tree seedlings which his brother would plant by a sheltering boulder in the centre of the garden. Kayin watered them carefully twice a day, dreaming of fluttering groves of aromatic leaves, even though the seedlings usually withered and died. One olive tree had taken root, however, and had grown to knee-height at the time of the story's beginning, sending out three slender branches.

Even though Kayin's father and mother liked his

garden, he knew that it grieved and dissatisfied them in some way. When the day's work was done, the family would sit together in the firelight, watching the moon rise above the hills and listening to the wolves howling on the plains. Then Kayin's father would look out at the garden and sigh.

'What is it, Father?' As Kayin asked, he knew the answer, because it was always the same.

'Ah, son, your garden stirs memories. Now I remember a garden...'

'What garden? Where?' Hevel would forget that he had heard the story before and would grow as excited as if his father were telling it for the very first time.

'A garden so great that it had its own mountains, its own valleys and waterfalls. Rivers turning to falling smoke and thunder and then deep, deep clear pools with glittering stones at the bottom. Even the fish in the water shone like silver and red gold. You nurse your little trees, Kayin, but in that garden were forests so high that I used to think they touched the clouds. And in the glades were fig trees, vines, pomegranates—and the fruit fell from the branches into your hands as you walked by.'

Glancing up from the fire, their mother added, 'I remember the white gazelles so tame that they came when I called and let me ride on their backs, and the spotted leopards who used to lie up among the branches and laze in the sun.'

'Where is the garden? Can we go to it too?' By then Hevel would jump to his feet, eager to be off.

Their father shook his head sadly. 'The way is lost. We could not find it again.' Kayin noticed how his parents' eyes would meet to exchange a reproachful look—no more than that, after year upon year of regret.

The old man paused for so long, his eyes closed, that I thought he had fallen asleep and I was about to lean forward and touch his shoulder. Then he moved, wiping what might have been a tear from his cheek.

'I am tired, my boy. Tired and too old to find the telling of such a long, painful tale an easy matter. Come back when I have rested a while, if thou canst leave thy other duties, and I will continue.'

'So this is the tale of how you came by your scar?' I asked.

The old man chuckled faintly. 'Impatient boy! Yes, it is the same tale. I have pondered it over and over again and I see clearly now how it all began with Kayin growing weary of hearing how much better life had been in the past; weary of having his beloved garden belittled through comparison with what was gone.'

3

Sacrifices

I spent some time praying alone in my cell that morning, according to our rule, after breaking my fast with the bread which the old man had refused. Nothing disturbed the usual calm of our little community. If the other brothers were curious about the pilgrim, they did not show it. As the quiet hours passed, however, I found it harder and harder to concentrate on my meditations. My thoughts kept straying to the tale that the old man had begun and long before noon I made excuses to myself that I should attend my charge. So, instead of joining the other brothers in the oratory, I hurried across to his small cell.

The old man was sipping water from the earthenware cup I had left by the bed but he shook his head when I offered to bring him some food.

'I need even less than thee and thy brothers who lead such a frugal life here,' he said. 'Besides, why eat when there is such a tale ripe for the telling? Sit down, sit down, son. I can see thou art impatient to hear more.'

'I am a man of prayer, Father,' I said, perhaps rather self-righteously. 'I cannot spare too many hours from my duties.'

The old man laughed. 'Well, the next part of my tale

concerns prayer. Do not think the family were not godly folk merely because they lived long ago.'

They too worshipped a god, knowing Him as El, Mighty One. Each day at sunrise and sunset the family stood on the plateau and prostrated themselves, while the father and mother called on the name of El and sang a hymn of dedication:

'Night and day,
Summer and winter,
Thou art Almighty
And we are Thy people
And we offer ourselves to Thee.'

While Kayin knelt down obediently beside his mother, Hevel always refused to prostrate himself, insisting that he could only worship standing upright with face and arms lifted to the sky. When they finished singing the hymn of dedication, he would dance sometimes, clapping his hands and kicking up his heels, shouting the name of El, despite his parents' attempts to reprimand what they considered to be unfitting behaviour. Hevel said that whenever he thought of El, his feet told him to dance. Kayin secretly sighed at his brother's nonsense.

One spring evening, not long before the grain harvest, the boys' father called them aside, saying that he must discuss important matters with them. Leaving their mother tending the cooking-fire in the cave, the brothers followed their father across the little plateau where the crops were ripening, past the caves where the flocks were penned for the night, and up a steep path winding to the summit of one of the surrounding hills. Climbing behind his father, Kayin noticed how the back of his neck was burned dark leathery brown by years of labour under the sun. His father was ageing fast, his hair grizzled, his shoulders bowed, his arms growing lean so that the muscles stood out like knotted cord. Perhaps the time was coming soon when he would finally relinquish all his work to his sons. Behind him, Kayin could hear Hevel humming tunelessly to himself. Any such changes would make no difference to Hevel who was already used to obeying Kayin's orders.

When they reached the top, they sank panting onto the grass which was lush and green after the succession of rainy winter months. A cloud of flies buzzed about Kayin's head and he swiped them away lazily. His father appeared to be surveying the empty hills which lay about them, and peering further off at the ragged outline of the western mountains.

Eventually he turned back to his sons and broke his silence. 'Kayin and Hevel, my only children, harvest-time approaches again.' He paused and Kayin looked up expectantly. Hevel was searching the grass for a grasshopper which had started its rasping song.

'We worship El together,' their father continued, frowning at the ground and seeming to test each word before he spoke it. 'The time is approaching when you must begin worshipping Him in your own right. We—your mother and I—can no longer be responsible for you.' He plucked at the short grasses with nervous fingers. 'When harvest comes, the time will be right. You must each go alone into the hills and dedicate yourselves to El. Take a gift with you, something your heart prizes above all else, and lay it before El on a high place. If you ask, He will give you a sign that He accepts your offering. Maybe—yes, you must ask for fire to come from the sky and consume it. In this way the gift will be both given and received and you will see that it is so. Do you understand?'

Hevel, holding the captive grasshopper in his cupped hands, nodded solemnly. 'A gift, a gift for El. That is a good thing.'

'Kayin?'

Kayin knew his father was waiting anxiously for his agreement, but suddenly his mind filled with questions. 'What has El done for me that I must make Him a costly sacrifice? You say it must be something I prize above all else? But what has He given me? Why can I not continue worshipping Him just as before?'

'Kayin!' His father rose to his feet, astonished. 'Everything we have comes from El, as I have told you many times. We are not owners, merely guardians. Even your skills in tending your garden are gifts from His generous hand. You must offer yourself unreservedly in return.'

'And the gift? How will I know what I should give?'

'Your heart will tell you when the time comes—but I shall not speak further about it now. When the time comes, you will know.' And his father turned the talk to other matters until the sun dipped below the horizon and they set off homeward for the evening meal and the customary prayers.

To Kayin the days seemed to pass more swiftly after that, the barley and wheat turning fat and golden almost before his eyes, and he started shaping a new flint harvesting sickle. Then one morning, his mother shook him awake before dawn, telling him to rise, dress and leave for the hills at once.

He stared at her sleepily, squinting in the light of the tallow lamp she carried. 'What are you saying?'

'Go quickly and take your gift. Go into the hills before the sun rises. The time for dedicating yourself has come.'

'Why must I go so early?'

'You have to leave before your brother wakes or else he will follow you. Now listen—when you leave here, walk eastwards and I will tell Hevel to go west. You must be sure to go alone.'

As Kayin knotted his loincloth and drew a cloak round his shoulders, his mother continued to whisper instructions. He had to go half a day's journey from the cave and find a place to shelter. Then he should wait until he received the sign of El's acceptance.

'And here,' she thrust a bundle into his hands. 'Meat and drink. If nothing has happened after three days, return home. But Kayin,' she rested a hand lightly on his head, 'if you call on El, He will answer. Be sure of that. And do not be impatient, my son.'

Stepping out of the cave, Kayin glanced back to where his brother lay, still sleeping, and wondered what sort of gift Hevel would take. A handful of coloured stones, perhaps, or a bright feather. Almost every day Hevel found what he thought of as treasures which he would gloat over and keep clenched in his fist until he dropped them or found something new.

Outside the cave, shadows still hid the plateau but there was light enough for Kayin to walk the paths of his garden, wondering what he should take. Of course, he thought, he should save the best of the crops for the family's food during the winter. More importantly, he needed to set aside enough as seed for the next year's planting. All the flowers were still tightly furled and he touched the wet petals lightly, wondering whether he prized them sufficiently to offer them up. Again, he would have to be careful and leave enough to make sure the garden blossomed even more beautifully in the following spring.

A turning of the path brought him to the centre of the garden where the boulder guarded his tree seedlings. The little olive tree rose above the rest, spreading its sturdy branches over the other frail twigs sprouting from the soil. Kayin caressed the trunk thoughtfully. If he cared for it well enough, it might even produce a crop of fruit one day. He decided to pluck a few leaves as part of his offering. Hurrying back through the garden, he gathered a small handful of flowers and wove them into a garland along with a spray of wheat and a few drooping barley heads.

'Kayin!' His mother was calling him from the mouth of the cave, pointing at the brightening sky. 'You must be gone now or you will be too late!' Shouldering his bundle, Kayin turned to the east where the sun burned red below the horizon. With a single glance back to where his mother stood, he set off.

By noon he had left the plateau far behind after hours of picking a way between the hills, only stopping to drink from a stream which rippled among the rocks of an old riverbed. He had not found any caves where he could shelter and so decided to settle himself on a patch of level ground, kindling a fire with dried dung to keep wild animals at bay. The air was quite still, so that he could hear the rasp of his bare feet on the grass, and the sun stood at the very zenith of the blue sky. Laying down his bundle, he built a circle of stones to contain his fire and then sat back on his heels, considering what he could do next. His father had said they should make their offering on a high place. On his left-hand side rose a smooth hillock which seemed high enough. He wondered whether he should start calling on El immediately, or whether He only heard petitions at the beginning and end of the day. His mother had said the time had come now. Carefully, he unwrapped the sacrificial garland from his bundle and set off up the slope.

Somehow the silence was even more profound when he reached the top. After a moment's thought he straightened the crumpled leaves and stems of his offering, spread it out in the exact centre of a patch of soft grass and prostrated himself beside it, his eyes screwed tightly shut.

Perhaps, he thought, he should say some words of dedication. Licking his lips, he muttered, 'El, I call on Thee to accept my sacrifice. It is the best of what I have and I offer it to Thee. Send me a sign that Thou dost accept it.' There was silence. Red and green dots danced before his closed eyes and his breath came short and hard.

He tried again. 'El, hear my words now. I know that everything I have comes from Thee. Accept what my own hands have grown. Send down fire and take this gift to Thyself.' Still silence, and a sudden agonising cramp in his shoulders which made him straighten up with a grimace.

The afternoon passed very slowly, the sun stubbornly fixed halfway down to the western horizon. Kayin lost count of the number of times he stretched himself face down on the ground and proferred his gift to an indifferent sky. When daylight finally darkened to dusk, he stumbled back to where he had made camp, trying to swallow a growing sense of hopelessness.

The next day passed in the same way, and the next, and on the evening of the third day, he decided to abandon his attempts. Lighting his own fire with the last of his fuel, he threw the drooping offering into the flames with great bitterness. A thin rain was falling. Determined not to spend another night at the place of his failure, he set off homewards in the darkness and limped back onto the plateau at daybreak. Above all else, he felt shamed and angry. He had done exactly as his father and mother had told him, but El had not answered. Dreading a painful encounter with his parents, he did not return to the cave and went to walk the paths of his garden as a garish dawn lit the eastern sky. He told himself that he would go and sit by the boulder, to look at his olive tree and soothe his wounded spirits.

As the light increased, he noticed something strange, something changed, about the garden. Something was missing. The first rays of the sun shot over the edge of the plateau and he saw that the olive tree was gone. The trunk was snapped off short, leaving a fragment of splintered wood protruding from the soil.

'Kayin!'

Dazed, he turned his head and saw Hevel running towards him. Although his brother's face was white with exhaustion, it was split by a huge grin. Rushing up to where Kayin stood, he seized his hand.

'Kayin! Listen to what happened to me!' Then he caught sight of the remains of the olive tree and fell into guilty silence.

Burning with fury, Kayin gripped his brother by the shoulders and shook him until his teeth rattled. 'You know about this, do you not? Tell me, tell me what you did!'

Terrified, Hevel gasped, 'But—but it was wood. I needed wood for the burning. I came back when nobody was looking, not even El.'

'How could you dare to touch my tree?' Kayin raged.

Hevel began to snivel. 'The gifts, the gifts for El. I

needed fuel to make them burn and I remembered the olive tree. El will give you other trees, Kayin.'

'You big fool.' Kayin's anger boiled inside him. 'The fire was supposed to come from El Himself, a sign that He accepted your gift. You did not need wood. And what did you take to offer? A heap of pretty stones? A handful of weeds?'

Hevel hung his head. 'I thought it was a love-gift, the finest things we could offer. I took the four best born of our flocks, only to please El.'

Kayin fought against the urge to strike his brother. 'Do you think El will be pleased if we waste our finest animals, the ones we need to make our flocks even better in the coming years? You are an even bigger fool than I thought.'

Hevel raised his wet face, his mouth working excitedly. 'But He was pleased, Kayin! Listen to how it happened. I went away into the hills and stayed there as we were told. It was cold and sometimes I was afraid, but I knew I should wait till El answered me. And it was last night, the last night I could wait, when I danced and sang one more time. And it happened.'

'What happened?'

'The great bright fire. Did you not see it? Coming down from the sky like lightning, and a noise like thunder and smoke all around me. When I looked again, the dead animals and the wood were burned away, and not even ashes were left. I was so glad that I ran back here, running all night, to tell you.'

4

The Way of Rebellion

As soon as Hevel finished telling Kayin his story, he ran to the cave and woke their father and mother whose faces shone almost as bright as his when they heard the news. Kayin saw the three of them standing together, hugging one another, as he wearily dragged himself to the entrance.

'And here is my other son!' his mother greeted him, her arms spread wide. 'Did El answer your prayers also?' Kayin returned the embrace unwillingly.

'I need food and drink,' he said, ignoring her question. 'Is there nothing for us to eat?'

'But Kayin,' his father took his arm, 'surely you have good news for us first?'

Kayin twisted away, picturing to himself their disappointed faces when they heard his tale.

'Yes, you must tell us, Kayin.' Hevel pressed against him affectionately. 'I want to know it all and you have said nothing.'

Driven at that moment to desperation, Kayin decided to lie. He could not bear to admit that he had been bettered by his younger brother.

'Yes, yes, it happened for me too,' he said hastily. 'I

saw the fire coming from the sky and it burned my offering completely, even though everything was soaked with morning dew. There was a sound like thunder too and I thought it might be El's voice.' His father and mother burst into relieved, happy laughter and Hevel gave a whoop of delight.

'Now you and me, we both belong to El's people,' he cried.

Kayin forced a smile of agreement and clasped his brother's outstretched hands. Inwardly, he choked with humiliation and resentment.

Three days later, he went in secret to the hills, looking for the place where Hevel had made his sacrifice. It was not hard to find. Kayin had half-hoped to see some proof that his younger brother had also lied; perhaps some charred animal remains and a pile of blackened olive branches, debris from Hevel's attempt to set fire to his offering. On his return he would take Hevel aside, tell him quietly that his deception was exposed and suggest that they both admit the truth to their parents. What he found instead was baffling: a hilltop scorched bare without a single trace of animal flesh or even bone. It looked as if the flames had licked round the summit in a perfect circle, leaving unscathed the grass growing along the very border of the burned patch.

Kayin stood on the baked soil and felt anger inside him, like phlegm in his throat. He spat and watched the tiny damp patch darken the ground, wondering what Hevel's feelings had been as he stood in that same spot a few nights before. Perhaps he had watched the white fire splintering through the sky and landing at his feet without harming a hair of his head. His brother was so sure of El that he did not need such signs. It was always Kayin who had wondered, who had questioned.

'Why not me?' Kayin asked aloud. 'Why Hevel and not me? Even though he spoiled the garden...' He thought of the gap by the boulder where the olive tree had risen so small and proud. His father had grieved for his sake too, shaking his head over Hevel's recklessness.

'Ah well, my son,' he said eventually. 'There will be other trees. Do not brood too long on what cannot be mended.'

Kayin gritted his teeth, remembering his father's words. How could he help brooding? Hevel was always excused for carelessly trampling things precious to his brother and nobody ever spoke of fairness or justice. Now it seemed that El Himself took no account of wrongs done to Kayin and granted his favours to an idiot.

The sense of injustice haunted Kayin as the family began the task of harvesting their crops. For several days they worked at threshing and winnowing the grain on a rocky outcrop at the edge of the plateau, where the wind blew aside the straw and a steady golden rain of plump kernels fell to the ground. Hevel sang as he laboured, the muscles in his bare back tensing as he swung the heavy threshing stick. Although the sweat trickled between his shoulder blades, he did not tire until long after the others stopped, panting, for a rest. Kayin shaded his eyes against the sunlight, watching his brother's face glow with happiness, the smile just a little vacant and the eyes slightly unfocused. Kayin knew his own wits were sharper, keen as a freshly-worked stone blade, but he felt that Hevel had some special brightness now, a new gracefulness in his movements, a joyful lilt in his voice.

Perhaps, he said to himself resentfully, *perhaps it is the blessing of El. Nothing for me, though. No favour or blessing for me.*

As harvest ended and the sun burned hotter, bleaching the grass yellow and drying the streams to mere threads of water, the brothers' parents began to notice how their younger son was prospering. The flocks in his care thrived despite the loss of the four finest animals in the spring, and many lambs and kids were born. Hevel himself was changing, understanding Kayin's orders at the first time of hearing, and noticing sooner when animals went sick or lame. His hands proved adept at splinting injured limbs or binding split hoofs, and it was Hevel who pounded the bark of one of the bushy shrubs growing on the plateau, and found it quickly halted the scour which had sometimes ravaged the flocks in the past.

Kayin noted how his father and mother praised Hevel, exclaiming how generously El showered blessings on His children, and as Hevel heard their praises, his face brightened and took on a kind of dignity, even wisdom. When his parents' eyes passed to Kayin, he guessed their thoughts easily. Why was El not blessing their older son likewise?

While Hevel prospered, Kayin felt as if something blighted his days. Time dragged by in a series of dull chores and his garden lay drab and summer brown, and he could not even rouse himself to plan and dream for the new year's planting as he used to do. After a while he could not bear even to look at Hevel's happy face and began feigning deafness when his brother spoke to him. Hevel appeared concerned about him, adding guilt to Kayin's burden of jealousy. Beneath the jealousy was shame because, for as long as he could remember, Kayin had been Hevel's protector, thinking and speaking for them both. Gradually, as the summer passed, the resentment and guilt and jealousy and shame became hate.

An evening came when Kayin saw for the first time how hatred had grown inside him like a poisonous weed. It was an evening little different from hundreds of others. The family had eaten a meal of parched corn and lentil pottage together, tired after hours of labour in the hot sun, and then each turned to the smaller tasks saved for the end of the day. Kayin's mother threaded goat hair onto a loom to weave winter cloaks and his father put a few more stitches into a pair of sandals. Hevel bent over a fragment of bone which he was smoothing with a sharpened stone before threading it onto a leather thong as a pendant. Kayin had shown him how to do that during the previous winter and ever since then Hevel had delighted in wearing as many as four pendants slung round his neck.

Kayin sat near the cave entrance, idly twirling a broken arrow in his fingers and watching his family. His mother caught his eye and gave him a quick smile, but the deepening lines on her forehead showed she was worried about him. Suddenly he seemed to see them from a great distance, across a shadowy abyss. They were sitting secure together in a circle of lamplight and he was far away, shut on the outside. Something twisted inside him, like a spasm of physical pain, and he caught his breath. He hated them, hated them so fiercely that he wanted to smash their safe circle, smash each one of them until he was left alone and free. Unable to sit still any longer, he dropped the arrow and ran out into the twilight.

He stood by the boulder in the middle of his garden, pressing his cheek against the cool stone and trying to calm himself. Without turning round, he knew that his mother had followed and was standing behind him.

'Kayin, what is troubling you so deeply?'

Struggling to steady his voice, Kayin said the first words that came to him. 'I am—I am still grieving about the olive tree.'

'Is that the whole truth of the matter, my son?' his mother said sternly. 'I think there is more. You must tell me.'

'That is all!' Kayin was angered by her probing.

'Listen to what I have to say,' his mother replied, 'and then see if you do not have more to tell me. I have been dreaming about you, Kayin, these past few nights. The same dream, again and again, and each time I wake up trembling, and my fear is always for you. Something terrible is hanging over you.' She closed her eyes, trying to recall exactly. 'The dream is only short, but it is always the same. I see you walking out of the cave, walking confidently with your head held high. Outside the cave is darkness and something is waiting for you in the darkness—something horrible, devouring—but you do not see it because you walk out of the cave so sure and confident, and when I call you in the dream, you do not hear me.'

Kayin involuntarily glanced over his shoulder to where night was gathering on the hills. A shudder ran down his back.

'Tell me what troubles you, Kayin.' His mother's persistence roused his temper.

'I cannot tell you what I do not know myself. Stop bothering me with your dreams. I am not a child any more, brought to order by a frightening story. Leave me alone!'

'Very well.'

Without another word, she went back to the cave,

leaving Kayin in the garden, forcing himself not to start at every shadow. When he was sure that the rest of the family had gone to bed, he returned and threw himself down beside Hevel, wrapping his arms around his head to shut out his brother's whisper, as Hevel begged him to say what was wrong.

At the very blackest hour of the night, Kayin woke suddenly. Beside him, Hevel moaned and moved uneasily in his sleep. The wind rattled the dry grasses out on the plateau and a breath of cool air strayed into the cave and brushed his face. In that same instant, he knew what he wanted to do, what he had to do. He had to kill his brother. Secretly, so that nobody knew what he had done, and carefully, so that it appeared to be an accident.

The old man faltered and he rubbed his watery eyes with a shaky hand.

'Why should he want to do such a terrible thing?' I asked.

'I have thought about it many times,' said the old man, and his words came weakly. 'I think I know why. He was the first-born and he was proud. He thought he had done right in making the offering he did to El, and when it was not accepted, he feared El wanted more than he was willing to give. And he saw his younger brother taking his parents' love from him.'

'And what did El want of him?'

'He did not discover that,' the old man said shortly.

As summer neared its end, Kayin thought constantly, night and day, about how he could carry out his task. He had to find a way of taking Hevel far away without attracting his parents' suspicion, and then contrive a deliberate accident of some kind. In the end it was his father who unwittingly sowed the seed of an idea which soon matured into a plan. He took Kayin aside and told him that he should go with his brother to look for a young tree to replace the lost olive.

'Hevel must learn to make amends,' he said. 'I know you loved your tree.'

Kayin nodded, silenced by the possibilities that his mind conjured up.

One day, when the clouded sky heralded the onset of the rainy months, Kayin got permission from his father to go into the hills for the day—he and Hevel together. He sensed his mother's gaze as she stood at the cave entrance, watching her sons leave the plateau, and made himself turn and wave farewell when Hevel did.

The brothers walked in single file, Kayin leading the way, until it was almost noon. Hevel had been talkative at first, chattering happily about all the beautiful trees he would find, but Kayin did not reply and eventually Hevel fell quiet. Realising that time was passing, Kayin walked faster, taking a route which led to the heart of the hills.

Hevel plucked at his brother's hand. 'Why this way, Kayin? I found more trees on the plains. The plains are the other way.' When Kayin took no notice, he stopped and sat down.

'Get up. We have much further to go,' said Kayin irritably.

'But I am tired. I need to rest. And we are going the wrong way.' Hevel rolled over and sprawled full length on the dusty ground. Eyeing him thoughtfully, Kayin knew he could not match his brother's strength and would only be able to attack him by stealth. Maybe the time had come. After so many days of scheming, emotion was swallowed up in the bloody excitement and cunning of the hunt. Hevel lay with his eyes closed, basking in the sun which had escaped from behind the clouds, dappling the world with shadows.

'Do you not think the sun is like El's smile, Kayin?'

'Of course,' Kayin answered, his hand closing on a large rock.

'The sun is good when it is not so hot,' Hevel went on happily.

Kayin lifted the rock in both hands and crept forward until he stood directly behind his brother.

'El's smile, you say?' he snarled, unable to resist a moment of gloating triumph. 'It is a pity El cannot save you now.' He swung the rock high in the air.

Hevel's eyes flew open and he screamed, once. Kayin struck hard and accurately, and carried on hitting until the familiar, foolish face was obliterated and the big body lay still, crumpled on the reddened earth.

5

Cataclysm

When his frenzy had spent itself, Kayin stood panting above his brother's broken body. Slowly his gaze moved from the corpse to his hands which still clutched the rock. Blood everywhere: his fingers, his forearms, even his face stiff and sticky and his feet sliding on crimson mud.

What had he done?

Panic seized him. Throwing down the rock, he ran on trembling legs, looking for somewhere to clean himself. He found a tiny pool not far from where the body lay, and plunged his head into the water until he had to come up, gasping for air. Snatching handfuls of gritty soil from the bottom, he scoured himself until his skin was raw and the water turned red. He tore off his loincloth and ran naked back to the body, hoping to rub away some of the blood on the ground. When he saw the piteous remains of Hevel, he began whimpering aloud, half in fear and half in an anguish of horror at what he had done. Dropping the loincloth, he grovelled on the earth, tearing at his hair and rocking backwards and forwards.

After a long, black moment, his thoughts started to clear. He drew a deep breath and sat up. What had his plan been before the blood frenzy overtook him? Wild animals. He was going to say that wild animals had killed his brother, so that it looked like an accident. Getting to his feet, he forced himself to look at the scene before him. The wet ground was churned by his footprints and the battered corpse still oozed a dark pool, although as he watched, it thickened and turned sluggish. Grabbing his loincloth, he wrung out the water to try to wash away the stain on the soil, but it only spread further. Then he set to work grinding his footmarks into slush so that all traces of his presence would be obliterated, desperately rehearsing what he would say to his father and mother.

'Torn apart by wild animals. We were separated in the hills and Hevel was lost. I saw blood, blood everywhere, and I was afraid so I ran away. An accident. It was an accident.' He gabbled the words over and over again until they were meaningless.

But how could he look his parents in the face and calmly tell such a great lie when the truth, hammering in his head, was that he had murdered his brother?

Then, for the first time, he felt descend upon him the full terror of the fugitive, the marked man. Abandoning his attempt to cover his traces, he fled blindly, arms flailing, until his strength gave out and he fell, choking and exhausted, on the rim of a plateau which opened out between two hills.

For a while there was no sound except for his laboured breathing. Then he heard a voice, a small quiet voice.

'Where is your brother?'

Kayin's heart pounded in his ears and he could not open his mouth. After a pause the voice came again.

'Where is your brother?'

Sweat sprang out on Kayin's body and he shivered. Forcing his courage, he raised his head to confront his accuser. He saw nobody there. Nothing except clouds gathering over an expanse of ground dotted with clumps of grass and forlorn, wilted bushes. He could not see where the voice was coming from.

'Who are you?' The words stuck in his throat.

'El,' the voice murmured.

Kayin's knees shook, but still he could see nothing except the hilly world which he had known all his life. The voice was surely that of his own guilt accusing him. The thought gave him a little more courage.

'Where are you?' he asked boldly.

'I am,' the voice replied. 'I am everywhere. Where is your brother?'

Kayin bit on his hand to stop himself from screaming. *I must be calm,* he said to himself. *I must not be afraid. If I stay quite still and stop myself even from thinking, the voice will go away.*

'Where is your brother?'

'Where is your brother?'

'Where is your brother?'

The question came again and again, like water dripping on a stone, until Kayin could bear it no longer.

'I tell you I don't know. I don't keep him tethered at my side.' His voice was a hoarse shriek.

'What have you done?'

'What have you done?'

'What have you done?'

'What have you done?'

Kayin writhed on the ground, blocking his ears with his fingers, but the voice did not relent.

'What have you done?'

'You know! You know what I've done!' he screamed at last, faint with terror.

'I see blood on the ground.' The voice sounded sad. 'It is your brother's blood. It cries out for justice.'

'Spare... me,' was all Kayin could whimper.

'You showed no mercy to your brother. Listen to me, Kayin. From this time on, wherever you set foot, you will carry the taint of what you have done. The ground where you tread will be stained with blood. It will never be fruitful for you. You will be a wanderer over the face of the earth, never at rest. You took your brother's life before he reached the full flowering of age, so your doom is to suffer likewise, never seeing your work come to fruition.'

Kayin felt a last desperate fury burn inside him, and dragging himself upright he shouted at the blackening sky, 'Then destroy me now if you are setting a curse on me. I will not be an exile, for ever fearing that someone will discover my deed and put me to death in punishment!'

The voice came remote through the first rumbles of the storm. 'I will set my mark on you and no one will touch you.'

The air grew hotter, throbbing with pent-up energy, as violet stormclouds mushroomed over the plateau. Lightning flickered over the ringing hills and stabbed the ground. When it flickered again, closer than before, Kayin felt the hair rising on his head. Then the lightning caught one of the nearby bushes so that it flared up like a torch. Without another thought, Kayin began to run, swift and desperate as a hunter's prey. Thunder crashed around him, louder and louder, as if the earth itself were cracking, while the tongues of fire ripped the clouds apart, burning the grass at his very heels. Kayin ran faster, tumbling over the far edge of the plateau and up the hillside beyond. *If I can only escape from the storm,* he said to himself, *I will be safe.*

Suddenly the thunder exploded right above, deafening

him. He caught his breath, and terribly bright fire was blazing around him, searing his skin. He felt as if his whole body were aflame, and he heard himself cry out in an odd, quavering voice before blackness took him.

The rain fell in cataracts, drenching the parched land and gradually lifting the weight of the storm from the sky. Slowly the deluge grew gentler and the tumult hushed. A gleam of sun shone through a gash in the clouds.

Kayin lay naked, blackened and helpless, barely conscious that the storm had passed. The rain had extinguished the fire, but he felt as if his own spark of life had been quenched as well. Too weak to move, he buried his face in the sodden grass and wept.

6

Brand from the Burning

In the first days after the storm, Kayin wandered like a madman, delirious with fear and pain, stumbling and straying in empty places. He came to his senses one bleak forenoon and found himself by a rock in a narrow valley, hungry, bruised and chilled to the bone. From then on he skulked in the hills, shivering in the rain which fell in a constant, slow weeping from the grey sky. He had no more than a few pitiful rags to cover himself and nothing to eat except what he could scavenge from the plateaus and valleys, but he did not dare return home. He tried to fill his stomach with handfuls of grass and shrivelled leaves and lapped water from pools like a wild animal. The rains fell day after day, soaking the ground so that he could not find a single twig of dry kindling for lighting a fire. Wolves or jackals could have set upon him as he slept undefended, but to his surprise he saw no other living creatures in his wanderings, although as he grew hungrier, he spent hours searching for tracks of the wild goats that lived in the hills.

Sometimes he got lost, but he knew the greater part of the land well enough to find a way back to familiar places before too long, always taking care to skirt wide round the part where his brother's body had been. He had seen the vultures circling the spot, high in the clouded sky, and turned away with a shudder, unable to clear from his mind the picture of picked white bones scattered on the mud.

The nights were the worst—almost. Every time he slept, he woke screaming from a dream of the small quiet voice and the coming of the storm. But the mornings were the worst of all, when he first rose from where he had lain sleeping. The grass had always withered beneath him—proof that El's curse was so strong that the very touch of his body was deadly to living things. At first he allowed himself to hope each morning that nothing had happened, that he had woken from a nightmare, and he cried with renewed despair whenever he saw the ugly brown death mark scarring the newly-grown grass.

Time passed in a blur of darkness and light, and gradually Kayin realised that he was starving. Strangely, he found that as he became weaker, his craving for bread and meat diminished and his thoughts grew more lucid. He knew that if he did not find food he would die. Despite knowing that he could not see his father and mother again, he was still certain, above all else, that he did not want to die. Standing on a bare hilltop, calculating his chances of survival as he shuddered with cold, he decided to risk a secret journey home.

He had no idea how long he had been out in the hills, although he saw from the sky that the rains were not over. Perhaps so many days had slipped by during his first delirium that two winters had passed since Hevel's death. He could not be sure. Travelling at twilight and taking remote ways far from where he might encounter his parents, Kayin drew nearer to his home plateau and the cave.

One dusky evening, at the very beginning of spring, he

stepped warily onto the plateau, ready to dart back into hiding at the first sign of his mother and father. All was empty and silent. More confidently, he approached the cave, seeing no flicker of firelight or rustle of movement from the smaller caves where the flocks were usually stabled. Then, as he drew closer, he realised that the caves were black and deserted.

Creeping into the entrance of what used to be his home, he saw the bare rock walls and floor, strewn here and there with animal droppings long since dried to dust. How long had he been away? Something sharp dug into his bare foot and he stopped and picked up a fragment of clay pot. Turning it over in his fingers, he wondered what had happened. Maybe they had left, looking for a new home, weeping for their sons, or maybe disaster had overtaken them, destroying them and all they owned. Perhaps El had extended the curse to blight Kayin's family as well. Too numbed even to cry, Kayin let the potsherd fall, and he looked about. At least he could spend the night there, sheltered from the cold and damp, and maybe the morning would bring him the wisdom to know what to do next. Scouring the corners of the cave, he found enough dry sticks to light a fire, and the flickering yellow light showed him a few stray kernels lying in the hollow where his mother used to grind grain. He tried roasting them in the embers and the scorched nutty taste took the edge off his hunger.

It was mid-morning before he woke, unaccustomed to the warmth of a roof over his head and free, for one night at least, from bad dreams. As he yawned and stretched, he noticed a broken hunting spear lying almost hidden in a shadowy recess. The stone blade was still keen and it only needed a new shaft to be a fine tool. Kayin weighed it in his hand and thought of fresh meat and smiled to himself. He would not die of hunger after all.

Taking the blade, he stepped outside and stared in bewilderment at the tangled brown wilderness rising where the garden and crops had once stood. Thorns and thistles sprouted thick where barley and wheat had flourished, and it was only too clear that everything Kayin had planted, every plant he had watered and cherished, had withered. With difficulty he found traces of the paths he had made so carefully and walked them for the last time. If he had not known, he could not have even guessed that a garden had once grown there. There was no sign of the trees he had planted by the boulder, and the stream which had watered the soil had shrunk to a single stagnant pool.

Suddenly Kayin halted, realising that he had not glimpsed his face since the lightning had burned him in the storm. Wincing at the memory, he bent over the pool, straining to see himself in the water. The sun emerged from behind the clouds, dazzling him, and then he saw clearly how the mark of El had changed him.

Kayin had never known whether he was handsome or not, although on the rare occasions when he did see his face he had thought it pleasing enough. What he now saw reflected in the pool almost made him cry out. A cruel web of red, raw scars crisscrossed his dark skin, as if the forked lightning had somehow stamped its pattern across him, blurring and twisting his features. The eyes stared back at him from hollow sockets and the mouth hung slack beneath painfully jutting cheekbones. Once, when he was very young, he had fallen against the cooking fire and burned his legs. When the wounds healed, he was left with two patches of tight, ridged skin, but the mark on his face was different. It was a hideous disfigurement, a merciless branding.

'A scar like a spider's web? Like yours?' I jumped to my feet, heedlessly interrupting the old man's tale.

He shook his head at me. 'Not so hasty. Wait patiently and the story will tell thee in due time. Now let me continue.'

Kayin drew back from the pool, sick at heart. He would search for some sign of what had happened to his father and mother, and then he would go.

'And I do not know where,' he shouted aloud, daring El to hear his voice. 'Thou hast set a curse on me to wander, so I shall fulfil it! Be satisfied with that and leave me alone.'

After searching the plateau, he found what he guessed to be the marks of an old trail, half-hidden by a new growth of grass. It could have been the route trampled by the flocks as his father drove them away. The trail was too faint to follow far and Kayin stood irresolute by the ruins of his garden, looking at the plateau. He had known nobody apart from his family and now he had lost them all, father, mother and brother, leaving him alone. Briefly, he remembered the evening when he had sat in the cave, longing to be free of them. His wish had been fulfilled more swiftly and bitterly than he could ever have guessed.

Where would he go? He hated the very sight of the hills now, so his path could only lead down to the plains where, as his father had once told him, a great river flowed and other peoples dwelt, scattered over the wide world. He flinched inwardly as he thought of strangers surveying him, unknown voices discussing him and his scarred face.

Clenching his fists, he willed the return of the cold determination he had felt in the hills. He would survive; he would not let his spirit weaken and fail and die.

First he needed meat and some kind of covering to shield him from the cold at night. Clutching the broken spear, he set off towards the lowlands beyond the plateau where he had seen wild goats straying in the past. After crawling through yards of wet undergrowth, he found three animals grazing together on the far sidc of a gully. His knuckles whitening on the fragment of spear shaft, he took aim and threw it as hard as he could, skewering the largest of the animals. Ignoring its death agony, he jumped across the gully and wrenched the spear out, but when the hot blood gushed from the wound over his feet and hands, and when he smelled the salty tang of it on the earth, he grew dizzy and nauseous. Staggering back, he fell to the ground, half-fainting, until his head cleared. Hunger forced him back to the dead animal even though he retched at the sight of the blood. Dragging it back to the home plateau, he lit a fire, butchered the goat and roasted it.

Burning his mouth on the hot meat, he thought how it was only the blood which so appalled him, not the death of the animal. His heart beat faster as he recalled the red stain on the grass and he shook his head to banish the memory. He would live, he would survive, and to survive he must kill and eat. Already he felt stronger.

He rested on the plateau for two more days, regaining his strength and making a crude cloak out of the goat hide which he scraped with a sharpened stone and stretched out to dry in the wind. After another hunting trip, he had enough hide to make himself a water-bottle and a simple pouch for carrying dried meat and a handful of dusty grain collected from the corners of the cave. Some of the grain he ground into flour and used for making a kind of hard biscuit which would last for days. As he watched it brown in the hot ashes, he remembered how his mother would bake it for him and his brother before they took the flocks to find fresh pasture in the dry summer months. The memory pained him so he crushed it deliberately, telling himself that the past was closed, finished. He could not return.

He left the plateau on the third morning just before dawn, walking steadily downhill to the great river plains which shone rich green in the first rays of the sun.

The sun rose and set more times than he could count as he travelled on, setting one foot before the other, watching the land become flat, and feeling the air growing warm and damp. Reeds and grasses rose higher than his head and he could smell the moist richness of the soil. At night he slept deeply, untroubled by any dreams, although before he lay down, he took care to enclose himself in a ring of little fires as a defence against wild animals. Sometimes he woke with a start and saw green or yellow eyes glowing at him in the darkness, but if he shouted and waved a smouldering stick, the eyes would wink out and he would hear the faintest rustle as the creature glided away.

Gradually, as the days went by, Kayin was able to put thoughts of the curse from his mind. The heavy air of the plains soothed him and made him sleepy and forgetful, and he no longer worried about where he was going or what he should do. The passing of night and day merged and changed so that sometimes he was walking on and on through an endless day, and at other times he opened his eyes and saw a night which seemed unbroken since the beginning of the world. Whole seasons bloomed and faded in the twinkling of an eye. He would feel the sun beating down on his head less fiercely and know that it must be winter, and then the rivers would rise to flood because spring had come again. He would sit and gaze at a blue flower in the palm of his hand and the moment would lengthen beyond any human lifespan. He ate when he was hungry and slept when he was tired, and still he saw the green grass dead beneath him when he woke, but by now it scarcely troubled him. He wandered on over the plains of the great rivers and time moved so strangely that he did not know how long he had been wandering nor even how old he was any more.

He was walking one morning, a stiflingly hot summer morning, when he saw smoke rising ahead of him. Astonished, he stopped short and began advancing as cautiously as a wild deer approaching a water-hole. Parting the tall grasses with the utmost care, he saw an extraordinary sight, something he had almost completely forgotten: a family. A young man with black hair curling to his shoulders was seated before a fire, while a brown girl knelt beside him, a baby tied snugly on her back. Behind them was a hut woven from bleached rushes. Drawing back, terrified that they might catch sight of him, Kayin ran until he felt safe. Then he sank to the ground, breathing hard, and considered what he should do. For a long time he thought about the scar he bore and the curse upon him, and the turmoil of his heart grew as he saw himself as others would see him—a fugitive, branded with the mark of his terrible deed. Better to wander on alone, far from other people, keeping his secret hidden safe. How could he live among other men and women if the hand of El was against him?

Then for another, longer time he was still, listening to the wind in the tall grasses. A heron flew overhead on slow, grey wings. The thought came to him that perhaps he might have a little hope.

'Hope? For what?' he said aloud and his voice was gruff and strange because he had not spoken for so long.

He could hope for his life among men and women to begin again. There was no need to reveal his past, and if El was against him, then he could live without El. Maybe He was not known so far from Kayin's old home.

'So I have decided.' He stood up and stretched his stiff legs. 'I shall seek out those people. I am not afraid.'

Gathering his bundle and his spear, he set off towards the place where he had first seen the smoke. Before he had gone far, he smelled it again, but this time the wind that brought it to him also brought voices, a buzz of human activity. Full of curiosity, he went forward until he found himself on the edge of a clearing. The grasses had been beaten back and in the place where he had seen the single hut, there now rose a whole village.

7

The Kindred

Kayin gazed in bewilderment at the round mud-brick huts in the middle of the clearing. He was certain that he had not lost his way, yet he had seen no sign of such a large settlement earlier. Before he could glide back into the sheltering grass, a small brown boy ran out from behind one of the huts and caught sight of him. He stared at Kayin, his eyes almost starting out of his head, and then rushed back the way he had come, screaming. Soon a whole crowd of people had hurried out, all staring at Kayin and whispering to one another behind their hands. Dazed by the sight of more people than he had ever seen in his life, Kayin scanned their faces which shared a family likeness, wondering if he would see the first man and woman who had stood outside their hut with the baby.

The crowd parted deferentially and a very old, very upright man appeared, his white beard hanging to his waist. He walked to within an arm's reach of Kayin and scrutinised him coolly.

'Give me your name and lineage,' he said, to Kayin's relief using speech he understood.

'Kayin. My name is Kayin,' he answered hesitantly.

'Your father's name?' The old man's gaze was stony.

'My father...' Kayin stammered. 'My father is dead, I think. I lost my family. I am alone.'

'Lost your kin!' The old man frowned. 'All of them? What great war has caused such a disaster? We have heard nothing of it.' The assembled people behind him muttered and shook their heads doubtfully.

'It was a storm.' Kayin saw that he might be able to excuse himself with a half-truth. 'A terrible storm and my family were killed and fire came from the sky and burned me so that my face is scarred. When I came to myself, I could not even remember the names of my father and mother. I have been wandering alone since that day.' Some of the crowd gasped and he went on more boldly, 'I saw some of your people not long before, a man and a woman with a baby, and I meant to ask them for help, but I lost my way and could not find their hut again.'

'Explain your words. No one of the Kindred lives outside the village. Do not lie to me, Abu, the Eldest of our tribe!' The old man spoke angrily.

Kayin was stung by the accusation. 'It is the truth, I tell you! I saw one man and one woman by a single hut, and I went away to gather up my courage to speak to them, and when I came back I found this crowd of huts and people.'

Before Abu could answer, an elderly woman, almost as wrinkled and white-haired as the Eldest, hobbled out of the crowd.

'He speaks truly,' she said in a matter-of-fact way. 'He comes to us from the past, the world of the dead. He has seen the first father and mother, the eldest of all the Kindred. The mark on his face shows that he is one set apart.' Unexpectedly she bowed to the ground. 'Tell us your wisdom, Mighty One.' Both Abu and Kayin stared at her.

'You cannot speak aright this time, Seriah,' said Abu after an awkward silence. 'This Kayin cannot be a Mighty One. He is only a young man, although anyone can see the signs of suffering in his face. No one has yet come back to us from the world of the dead, and it would be one of our own fathers, not a stranger.'

'I always speak aright, but you do not believe me,' Seriah cried shrilly and stumped away, her mouth pursed.

Abu turned back to Kayin. 'She thinks you saw the first of our tribe, that you have come to us from the past. Sometimes she brings us wisdom about the days ahead or sees clearly into men's hearts, but sometimes she is confused.'

'And do you believe my story?' Kayin asked. Abu narrowed his eyes.

'I think,' he said eventually, 'that you have indeed lost your kin in some terrible disaster, but I think your heart is still troubled. The Kindred will take pity on you and give you food and shelter. Follow me.' He led Kayin through the throng of people who shrank back at their approach, evidently afraid of Kayin's touch.

Stooping to enter the low doorway of one of the huts, Abu pointed to a mat of woven rushes lying in one corner. 'You may rest here. One of the daughters will bring you food and drink later.'

Kayin had arrived at the village when the sun was already sinking westward and it was nearly dark before he heard a timid footstep outside and a young girl entered, carrying one bundle on her head and another in her arms. Setting down her loads, she unwrapped one and shyly proferred Kayin a thin cake of unleavened bread and a skin of soured milk. He ate and drank gratefully, watching as she unrolled a goat-hair blanket and spread it over the sleeping mat.

She was about to leave without speaking to him, when he put out a hand. 'Do not go without my thanks.'

'My father told me to bring these things.' She glanced at him from under her lashes.

'Tell me your name.' Kayin had never encountered anyone outside the circle of his family before; certainly no one like this bright-eyed, black-haired girl.

'Ani,' she told him, her confidence visibly growing. 'I am the sixth of my father's seven daughters.'

'Seven daughters!' Kayin had never imagined families so large.

'And two sons also. My father has three wives.' She looked at him inquisitively. 'They say you have forgotten your family.'

Kayin nodded without replying, marvelling at the way the last of the evening light spilled through the doorway and shone on the girl's hair so that it glistened like black oil. Ani met his gaze and blushed, turning and hurrying out of the hut before he spoke to her again.

Left alone, Kayin pondered what had happened, breathless after the sudden encounter with other people after such a stretch of solitude—and he puzzled over the words of old Seriah. Could it possibly be true, as she had declared, that he had somehow strayed through time? Or was it as the Eldest had said, that his heart and mind were troubled and confused? Kayin tossed uneasily on the rush sleeping mat, beginning to doubt his own story and unsure of whom or what to believe.

As the next days passed, he started to wonder whether he should have stayed out alone in the wilds, away from the complications of other lives. Whenever he appeared in the doorway of his hut, heads turned and he felt the people scrutinising his scar, staring unashamedly and remarking on him in his hearing. From time to time Abu or one of the other older men among the Kindred came to visit, often simply standing and watching him as he sat slumped on his mat.

'It is strange,' said Abu at one such visit. 'You look no older than my own sons, yet Seriah swears there is some mystery about you. My heart, too, tells me there is something strange. We shall see...'

'What have the dead to do with the living?' asked Kayin curiously. 'Do not the Kindred believe their lives are directed by...by a mighty spirit, one who demands their worship?' He could not bring himself to speak the name of El.

'A mighty spirit?' Abu sounded puzzled. 'Seriah says she dreams of Mighty Ones, men like giants, with bright, fierce faces and voices like thunder, but some of her dreams are foolish. The Kindred venerate the fathers who sleep in the earth—those who breathed their last and lie at rest outside the village, our hidden guardians. We bury them with honour and they watch over us. That is why the Kindred is growing to be a mighty people.'

It is not true. It cannot be true, Kayin said to himself. *The dead are—are dead, powerless. I must be strong. I must survive and never let out my secret. If nobody knows what I did, then it can never harm me.* But the fear still fluttered in his chest like a caged bird.

He guessed that his position in the village was a delicate one. He had already unsettled the people by provoking old Seriah into claiming near divinity for him, and perhaps Abu was worried that Kayin might be tempted to try and wrest power from his hands. Such an idea was so far from Kayin's own wishes as to seem almost amusing. Increasingly, as time passed, he felt that he had no place in the Kindred's lives. He watched them from his hut. The men farmed their crops and herds of goats and went hunting game on the plains. The women baked bread, wove lengths of black and brown cloth and raised playful hordes of children. Not only did the disfiguring mark single him out as different from the rest of them, but he dreaded that if he forgot the curse and tried his hand at sowing and reaping again, the living plants would wither under his fingers. Then the people would turn on him as a bringer of misfortune and wrest his secret from him, maybe even put him to death.

'As for the mark I carry, I do not believe it would protect me,' he said to himself bitterly. 'Why should El protect me any longer? I renounced Him and He has surely renounced me.'

Wandering disconsolately from the hut one morning, Kayin found he was nearing the clay-pit where the Kindred women made bricks and watertight linings for the crude rush baskets which they used for carrying water. He bent down and picked up a handful of the slimy red-brown clay drying in the fierce sun at the edge of the pit. Without thinking, he started working the stuff, kneading and squeezing it into different shapes. He had never worked clay before, but suddenly he felt as if new-found skill was tingling in his fingertips. Smiling, he looked at what he had made—a crude model of one of the long-legged goats which roamed the village. Perhaps he could make something for Ani; a gift to thank her for all the mornings and evenings she came to his hut with food and drink. Perhaps then she would stay and speak longer with him.

By the time of the village's noon rest when the Kindred took shelter from the heat, Kayin had made a row of small, round clay beads, each pierced through the middle with a splinter of bone. Leaving the little clay goat for one of the children to find, he carefully gathered up the beads in a rag and carried them to the women's quarters where the cooking fires were smouldering. He had already noticed how the broken bricks ringing the fire circles became hard as stone in the heat, and decided to bake the beads in the red-hot coals to harden them likewise. He was aware of curious faces watching him from dark doorways, but he did not look round. He was intent on what he was doing.

He gave the beads to Ani the next morning, threaded onto a string of hide and embellished with intricate patterns which he had painted with three hairs dipped in red ochre. Ani immediately tore off the bone pendant which was her only other ornament and laughed delightedly as Kayin fastened the new necklace around her neck. She danced off to show her mother and sisters and soon returned, boasting of their envy and begging him to show how he had made the beads.

Kayin found that once won, her friendship and confidence were unshakeable and wholehearted. She willingly lingered to talk with him, recounting the doings of her sisters and brothers, and escorting him round the village so that he could see the women repairing the flat roofs of the huts with fresh palm leaves and tightly-packed earth. She took him to the place where the girls wove rush baskets and along the path leading to the river where the boys speared fish. She also showed him the grove of fig trees which had been planted, so she had heard, by the first father and mother. Kayin stared at the swelling fruit, trying to forget the stump of a slender olive sapling in what had once been a garden high in the hills.

When Ani led him to a patch of bloodied, trampled ground where her uncle butchered his goats, Kayin felt his heart give a sudden sickening lurch and Ani's chattering voice sounded as if it were coming from far away.

'What is wrong?' She hovered anxiously beside him as he stumbled away.

'Nothing. That is, I cannot bear to see death after what happened to my family.'

Ani was instantly contrite. 'I was cruel to forget what happened to you. Forgive me, Kayin!'

He smiled at her concern. When he questioned her about where the dead were buried, she took him to the eastern outskirts of the village and pointed to a series of low mounds along a fallow field.

'This is where the Eldest of the Kindred is always buried. It is a sacred place,' she said. 'Only the Eldest can walk there, but he does not choose to do so often. He does not want to anger our fathers by trampling on their resting-places.'

'And the rest of your people? Where do they lie?'

'We bury them beneath the floors of the huts so they stay close to those they left behind.' Ani laughed at Kayin's frown of distaste at the idea.

In a little more than a day, the news of Kayin's clay-working spread throughout the Kindred and both men and women left their usual tasks and came to watch him. At first he made quantities of beads until Ani's sisters were decked out as proudly as she. Establishing a place for himself by the clay-pit, he mixed colours and textures, finding the best, hottest part of the fire for baking his handiwork. He tried to recall how his mother's skilful fingers had twisted the clay into coils to make cooking pots. The Kindred had only ever used their clay to daub rush baskets and make crumbling bricks, but now they abandoned their old water-carriers and eagerly bore off the pitchers Kayin shaped. He lavished the same care over each thing he made, decorating it with ochre or scratching out patterns with a fishbone.

Even before Abu told him that he could join the Kindred, Kayin knew he wanted to stay. His hands were gifted in a way he had never suspected, and sometimes he would examine them, delight welling up as he realised that he was a true craftsman, able to see and shape what nobody else could picture. Abu came to him one noon-time and examined Kayin's hands for himself.

'Some say there is strange magic in your hands,' he said. 'To me they are simply strong and work-hardened. I want you to stay with the Kindred, Kayin. The people hold you in high esteem already.' Kayin bowed deeply in reply, thanking the Eldest for his kind words and adding that nothing would gladden him more than staying at the village.

'I must warn you, though,' Abu paused on the threshold. 'You must tread carefully with my daughter. Her eyes are bright when they rest on you, but she is promised to her cousin.'

Kayin found he could not meet Abu's gaze. 'She is promised to her cousin?'

'Her cousin Kidu. We will celebrate the betrothal before the fig harvest.'

When Abu had gone, Kayin sat cross-legged on his mat, crumbling a ball of dried clay. He told himself that the Eldest did not hold him in any special regard; that he had no reason to expect the offer of his daughter as well as the invitation to join the Kindred. Yet he could not swallow his disappointment.

As the day of the betrothal drew near, Kayin occupied himself with clay-working, inventing new, beautiful patternings which the Kindred women started to copy in their weaving. Some of them decorated their plain rush sleeping mats with strands and stripes of colour. Not content with spending so many hours at the clay-pit, Kayin travelled out over the surrounding plains gathering roots and leaves which produced dyes of fresh greens and yellows, as well as a rich golden-brown. Ani's mother was occupied with making her daughter a fringed betrothal shawl and gladly accepted Kayin's handful of crushed leaves which turned the coarse cloth the colour of new green leaves.

Kayin deliberately kept away from Ani, angry with her for failing to tell him about her betrothal. Although he knew she watched him as he walked about the village, he never looked up and greeted her. When the betrothal day finally came, he saw her being led from her mother's hut to where the Kindred were assembled near the sacred burial ground. Staying on the outskirts of the crowd, he studied Ani's face. The women had reddened her lips, painted green shadows round her eyes and plaited strips of red cloth into her oiled hair. Somehow she did not look more beautiful, but merely like a sadder, older girl.

8

Pestilence

When the feasting for Ani's betrothal and the fig harvest were both long passed, the village lay quiet under the winter rains for many days. Kayin set aside his pot-making for a while and spent hours etching shapes onto pieces of soft clay using a finely-honed stone blade. He was sitting in his hut late one evening, idly drawing a row of dancing figures, when he heard scurrying footsteps nearby and hushed, urgent voices. Then a woman cried out in what he recognised was the Kindred's death wail.

Peering outside, he saw a woman approaching, muffled in a heavy cloak.

'Is something wrong?' he called softly. The woman did not stop, but Kayin caught her muffled reply as she disappeared round a corner.

'It is the pestilence returned. We will all be struck down.'

By the middle of the following morning, Kayin saw only too clearly what her warning meant. Overnight a deadly sickness had descended on the village of the Kindred, moving with terrible swiftness from hut to hut, snatching life from young and old alike in just a few hours. Kayin went in search of Abu to ask what was happening and found him kneeling grey-faced by the body of his youngest wife, Ani's mother.

'Go,' he said to Kayin. 'The pestilence will take you if you stay. Go while you are still strong. Save yourself. You do not have to share the fate of the Kindred.' When Kayin answered that he had nowhere else to go, Abu only shrugged helplessly.

He learned more from old Seriah who never seemed to be touched by any sickness as she stumped around the village, carrying pitchers of milk and water for the sick and loaves of barley bread for those who nursed them. She told Kayin that the pestilence had visited the Kindred before, sometimes taking no more than two or three of the oldest and weakest, sometimes raging like a hungry fire until whole families were wiped out.

'Many years go by without it coming and then it strikes hard,' she said in answer to his questioning. 'But even I cannot remember it coming as fierce and hungry as this time.'

Night and day the whimpers of the dying and the wailing of the mourners sounded in the village, and still the pestilence raged. The air was thick with the smoke of aromatic herbs, burned to hide the stench of the sickness. People whispered that the fathers were angry and had sent the pestilence to wipe out the village, so when he had buried his wife, Abu led the people in a ceremony of propitiation at the resting-place of the Kindred fathers, pouring steaming bowls of oil and blood over the grassy mounds. That very evening, Abu's first-born son fell ill. Kayin woke in the middle of the night and heard the death-wail go up louder than ever, mourning the loss of the Eldest's heir.

When daylight came, the village was unusually quiet.

On his way to the clay-pit, Kayin met Ani who told him that the people were keeping silence in honour of her dead brother.

'I grieve for him too,' said Kayin.

Ani kept her gaze averted. 'My father is in council with his advisers. Seriah has warned him that the Kindred will be utterly destroyed if they do not heed her words.'

'And what is she saying?' Kayin asked. Ani shook her head without replying and hurried back to the hut where her husband lay sick.

All day long Abu held council, only emerging from his hut when the evening shadows lengthened over the plains. Pale and exhausted, he summoned the people to the centre of the village. Kayin stood among the crowd, filled with pity at the broken state of the Kindred. Many were missing, many too weak to stand and those who remained in better health were worn out with sorrow and care.

'My people,' Abu began. 'My people, we suffer grievously.' There was a mutter of assent. 'Fearing that our fathers were angry, we tried in vain to placate them and since then we have suffered even more.' He stopped a moment, his face working with emotion. 'This very morning, Seriah brought words to us, words of knowledge, saying that we have indeed angered the fathers.' He flung both his arms in the air. 'Hear me, O Kindred! It was I who brought the pestilence upon you. It is I who am at fault, because I refused to believe the truth about the stranger who came among us; the stranger we now know as Kayin, our pot-maker.' Every eye turned on Kayin and he grew hot with dread at what the Eldest would say next.

'O my people,' Abu continued, 'I believe that Kayin does indeed come to us from the past, from the world of our dead fathers. He did indeed see the first father and mother, the eldest of all the Kindred. The word Seriah brought to us proclaims him as a Mighty One, a lord of wisdom. It is he who should rule over us!' Pushing his way through the crowd towards Kayin, he fell down before him and pressed his forehead to Kayin's foot. 'Hail, Mighty One, Eldest of the Kindred. Have pity on us!'

Kayin looked about and saw that the rest of the people were as astonished as he was. He tried to pull Abu to his feet but the old man only cried out, 'Have mercy, Lord! Spare me and my people!' Before Kayin could reply, two of Abu's advisers appeared beside him.

'We knew nothing of this,' one muttered to Kayin as they gently raised Abu who had fallen into some kind of fit. 'We think the loss of his son and his wife has turned his wits.'

'And he has another son,' Kayin said. 'Surely...' But the man silenced him with a shake of the head and turned to the buzzing, expectant crowd.

'The Eldest himself has fallen sick,' he announced and the people wailed. 'Hear me! His last words were confused. When we spoke in council, we agreed that our fathers brought Kayin to us, guiding his footsteps because they chose him to lead the Kindred to greatness. We sinned in not understanding why he had come—but this talk of Mighty Ones and passing through time is nonsense. The council of Abu agreed to set matters right by making Kayin heir, as if he were the Eldest's first-born son. He will become our lord when his adopted father dies. Which may be sooner than we thought,' he added in an undertone.

Kayin noticed a young man, scarcely older than a boy, slipping away from the back of the crowd. He recognised him as Abu's second son, and he was talking earnestly with two companions.

When the Kindred had dispersed to their huts, Kayin found Kish, the most senior of Abu's advisers, at his side, and he asked about the Eldest's second son.

'Surely he becomes heir after the death of his brother?' he finished.

'We debated the matter many times and Abu told us again and again that the younger lad is not fit to be a leader. He does not command the people's respect and has no authority. His father says he would try to satisfy his own desires instead of seeking the people's best interests. We see that you are not so.' Kish smiled at Kayin who tried to ignore the tide of shame rising in his heart.

It soon became clear that Abu had fallen victim to the pestilence, and although his end was not as swift as it was for some, he was dead before noon the next day. Kayin was at his side as he drew his last breaths and received his blessing and final commands.

'You must save the Kindred,' the old man murmured. 'Lay me with my fathers and then save my people. You must make them strong.'

They buried him at dusk, his body tied in the customary crouching position, his head placed on a white stone. A waterskin, a fishing spear and a basket of barley grain were laid round him so that he would have food and drink in the land of the dead, and under Kish's guidance Kayin placed the Eldest's horn-tipped staff in the dead hands before strewing the grave with powdered red ochre and singing a chant for the dead. As they returned to where the rest of the people waited, Abu's two surviving wives began weeping loudly, tearing at their hair and clothing, throwing themselves onto the ground and covering themselves in dust. The other women joined in and the whole village echoed to the clamour of their mourning for three days.

On the fourth morning, Kayin was woken by Kish crowding into his hut together with Abu's six other advisers, telling him in a hurried whisper that they had come to make him Eldest.

'The people must have a leader, but there is too much sickness and sorrow for a fitting celebration. We will feast when the pestilence is gone and make for you a staff of office, but we think it right that you should take the name of Eldest at once. The Kindred must see that Abu made a worthy choice for his heir.' Kayin nodded sleepy assent.

The seven men gathered round him in a circle and Kish spoke a little louder. 'We would have you lead us. We would have you be Eldest of our people. We would have you as lord.'

Kayin took a deep breath and answered in the way they had told him. 'Willingly.' The seven men bowed and Kayin bowed in return.

'And now, Eldest,' Kish went on, 'it is fitting that you should be betrothed. A girl has been set aside as the wife of the new lord and you inherit her as you inherited the ruling of the Kindred.'

'A wife! You said nothing about a wife!' Kayin protested, as two hooded women stepped into the hut, one shorter than the other. Kish came forward and led the shorter woman to Kayin, and he found his hand being pressed into hers.

'Take Nena as yours,' Kish said. 'May she serve you faithfully and bear you many sons.'

A wife, said Kayin to himself, and felt desire kindling inside him. Maybe her face would be as pretty as Ani's, her body as satisfyingly rounded. *I can take her,* he thought, *but I do not have to love her.*

Reaching out, he tentatively pulled the hood from his wife's face. He saw red cheeks, a trembling mouth, eyes shyly downcast so that he could not tell what she was feeling. He sensed the others filing out of the hut, leaving them alone together. The woman made a small, nervous sound.

'Please—do not be afraid,' Kayin said gently. 'This is as strange to me as it is to you. Till this moment I knew nothing about a wife.' She made no reply, but she did not flinch as he began running his fingers through her soft black hair.

9

City on a Hill

The pestilence continued to ravage the Kindred, with so many people dying that bodies lay unburied for days and the stink of decay poisoned the air. Kayin saw how few and weak the survivors were and gave orders for the corpses to be placed in a common grave outside the village. While some cried that such violation of tradition would anger the fathers, most saw the sense of Kayin's words and none dared disobey the command of the Eldest.

Kayin had little else to do at that time besides keeping a tally of the dead and overseeing the distribution of food to orphaned children. Nena proved to be a timid, obedient wife who devoted herself to caring for Kayin's needs. Since she spoke seldom, he welcomed her presence in his hut, enjoying her soft body whenever he pleased. According to custom, she would return to the women's quarters as soon as she was with child.

Kayin's duties were by no means taxing and he found he had plenty of time for worry and reflection. Lying awake at night, listening to Nena's quiet breathing, he pondered what he should do, wondering how he could prove himself an able leader of the Kindred. He knew he could not work the soil and had no inclination to make war on other tribes. What could he do? Although his sudden rise to power had shaken him at first, he exulted in his new authority and felt he could at last see the course of his life running straight and smooth. The task before him was to determine the kind of leader he could make and shape a vision to inspire his people.

During one moonless night, he had a vivid dream as he hovered between sleep and waking. He thought he was trudging up a steep hill with a group of men and women who were laughing and talking together.

'See how bright the city is!' said one, and Kayin lifted his eyes to the top of the hill and saw lofty stone walls gleaming like the sun. Through a pair of immense gates he glimpsed a wide road lined with huts also built of stone and towering like mountain peaks.

The memory of the dream was still fresh in his mind when morning came and he meditated on it, absently eating the food which Nena set before him. A city—not a village of dirty mud brick huts crumbling into dust, but fitting homes for craftsmen who used precious wood and stone to create beauty as he had once used earth to make a garden. He had never heard tell of any settlement so strong and proud as the city in his dream, but he saw it clearly in his mind's eye and could have described it as surely as if he had walked its ways all his life. It lingered in his thoughts for the rest of the day and that night the dream came again. This time he was closer to the top of the hill where the city gates opened in welcome.

I understand, he said to himself, still half in the dream. *It is the task that I must set the Kindred. They shall build a city for themselves.*

But how could he persuade the people to leave behind the burial-grounds of their fathers? He had learned not to tremble at the thought of the dead—nothing had come to haunt him, no cold, watchful presence in the night—but the Kindred were bound by custom and blood-loyalty to the old ideas. Kayin clenched his fists. He was Eldest now. He would prevail on them to leave behind the place of ghosts and go to a new home.

In the village the time of sickness was finally passing. One, two, three days went by without anyone falling ill or dying and the survivors emerged shakily from their beds, young men as weak and trembling as the oldest grandmother. As Kayin went about among his people, he sensed their brokenness. Nobody spoke of celebrating the end of the pestilence because so many had been lost. Entire families had been wiped out, leaving their huts empty and forlorn.

When a whole week had gone by and it was clear that the pestilence was really gone, Kayin summoned his advisers to a council. Only four men out of seven remained and they made a gloomy half-circle around Kayin who sat above them on a smooth white stone—the stone they would have placed beneath his head had he died and gone to lie with the Kindred fathers.

'Tell me your thoughts,' he said, looking at each of them in turn. 'What do you think I should do?'

After a heavy silence, Kish spoke. 'What hopes are left for the Kindred?'

'No hope,' Kish's brother Irad said after another silence. 'Others will come, strangers who will kill us or take us captive and the Kindred will be wiped out.'

'I have plans.' Kayin spoke more confidently than he felt, wondering whether his dream would sound as powerful told aloud to dispirited men. 'Wisdom came to me as I slept and brought me a plan for the Kindred. A way of lifting us higher than any other tribe.' He described the dream to them, and seeing their incomprehension he tried to explain what he had pictured. 'A city, a place like nothing ever seen before. Homes far bigger than our village huts and as many as the reeds on the plains. News of the Kindred's work would spread and other people would come, begging to join us. Soon we would be the greatest tribe in all the lands.'

'But we cannot leave our fathers' resting-place,' said Irad.

Kayin grew passionate as he saw his dream being thwarted. 'The fathers will be glad to see the Kindred growing so strong, and the old village will remain a holy place in their honour, tended by those men and women who wish to stay here.'

The four advisers sat speechless, their eyes fixed on Kayin, until he burst out, 'Answer me. Advise me. Is my plan wise or not?' Then Kish knelt down and the others followed his example, pressing their foreheads on the ground.

'So you approve what I say?' Kayin demanded, not daring to believe that they did so.

'You have been granted a vision.' Kish's voice was muffled as he remained prostrate. 'A vision from the fathers. Command us, Eldest and we will obey!'

The old man stopped and gave me a shrewd glance. 'Hast thou ever seen such a place, such a city, son? Thy face tells me that perhaps thou hast not.'

I sighed. 'I have never even visited the mainland. I was born on this island and have never left it once. Of course I hear tales about faraway cities, but...' I added piously, 'I prefer to meditate on the New Jerusalem, the city of God.'

The old man did not answer and I suddenly noticed that the sun was past noon. The hours had sped by as I listened to the story and I would have to answer to the brothers for so carelessly neglecting my prayer duties.

The old man seemed to read my thoughts because he sat up on his bed, saying fiercely, 'Thou shalt not leave! Thou shalt not leave until the tale is done. There can only be the one telling, and when it is done I can rest. Remember that if I die without making full confession, it will be because of thy neglect. Leave thy prayers for a while!'

'But are you not hungry?' I asked, blushing at his reproof. 'I could bring you something…'

The pilgrim cut short my offer impatiently. 'If thou art hungry, then eat. All I need is a little water.'

I gave him a brimming cup and he drank thirstily.

'Better!' he sighed, sinking back into the covers. 'Now listen well!'

Word of Kayin's plan spread swiftly from hut to hut and the people flocked to him, eager to hear more. After giving orders that some should continue tilling the fields so that the Kindred had enough food, he decreed that as many as possible—men, women and children—should devote themselves to founding the city. With his remaining advisers he found a few level, well-drained acres not far from the village and settled on those as a suitable site. Deciding the scale of the city was difficult. In Kayin's dream, it looked large enough to house all the nations of the world; far greater than the Kindred could ever build. Kish told him that there were forests in the northern mountains, but it would take many months to haul enough wood to build just a few huts.

But Kayin decided that the people could still use their

hands to create a home worthy for the great nation they could become, even if they simply embellished the clay bricks with white stones from the riverbed.

Sending six strong young men to fetch timber from the distant forests and another group to gather rocks, Kayin set about showing the rest of the people how to make fire-hardened bricks. He found Ani at his side again, begging him to set her a task, and he put her in charge of a busy company of women who produced ornamented blocks by packing wet clay into embossed moulds. While they waited for the timber and stone, the others dug foundations and built a strong perimeter fence of tightly-woven reeds. Within the walls, Kish built the first of many round houses—far larger and more spacious than the village huts—and Kayin decorated the doorway with inlays of chipped stone. Many days later, the six weary young men returned, dragging with them two long tree trunks, and Kayin worked with them in carving wooden lintels for the huts, embellished with interwoven patterns of fig leaves, wheatstems and running gazelles.

As the work proceeded, Kayin walked among the people, his new staff of office in his hand, and urged them to greater efforts. When he saw how willingly they worked, even in the oppressive heat of summer, he laughed in his heart, full of triumph. The terrible past—the curse, the despair—was left behind, and each day was gladder than the one before. Even his disfigured face did not matter any longer. The people were used to the sight of him and did not look away or turn to stare as he went by.

As they returned from the city site at nightfall, Kayin often found himself walking beside Ani, telling her of his longing to build bigger, more splendid cities, where the least brick was shaped as carefully as a fine cooking pot;

where paths of white sand led from house to house; where the flocks were stabled in dwellings fit for a village chief. They laughed together as his visions became fantastical—ovens so vast that the women could roast meat enough for a whole tribe, buildings soaring as high as the stars, a city with a river running through the very middle, banked by strange trees carved from glittering stone.

One evening, as they neared the village, Kayin was surprised to see Nena approaching. Leaving Ani, he walked quickly to meet her.

'You are well, my husband?' she asked.

Kayin looked hard at her, noticing a demure smile at the corners of her mouth. 'The city walls are finished and we are building good huts of baked brick for the women's quarters. The work goes so fast that we shall be living there by the end of the winter rains.'

'I am glad, Eldest.' She smiled at him openly. 'It is good that you are making us a new home because when the winter rains end, we shall be three. I am with child.'

Kayin gaped in disbelief. As he heard the news, he realised that in a secret corner of his heart, he had doubted that he would ever have children of his own. The curse upon him was not as far-reaching as he had feared. Suddenly gladness welled up inside him and spilled over, and he caught Nena in a joyful hug. 'That is good news! Very good news! If you give me a son, we will call him...' he thought for a moment, 'Kanoch, your grandfather's name. And listen, we will name the city, the new city, after him. He will grow to be the Eldest of the mightiest tribe ever seen in this land!'

10

Kanoch

Sooner than expected, the Kindred found word about their city spreading to other tribes who had until then kept themselves hidden in the southern marshlands, the western desert and the mountains to the north and east. Hunting parties from the village met strangers out on the plains, seeking the place which rumour described as the greatest stronghold ever built. One small clan presented themselves to Kayin, begging leave to join the Kindred.

'Once we were many,' their chief said. Kayin noted that although his face was wrinkled and blackened by years of journeying under the desert sun, his shoulders were still broad and strong. 'Then sickness came in the winter and we lost almost half our number.'

Kayin met in council with his advisers to discuss the matter. As he explained what the new clan wanted, the others looked wary.

'We are the Kindred, but how can our children bear the name proudly if their blood is mingled with that of strangers?' asked Irad cautiously.

'And maybe many people will come, perhaps meaning to attack us, if they hear that the Kindred give welcome to all,' Kish added.

'But if Abu had not welcomed me, the Kindred would not now have a city,' argued Kayin. 'Besides, we need many more hands to speed the building work.' Eventually he brought them to agree, reluctantly, that the clan could join the Kindred if they swore oaths of allegiance and submission to Kayin, and bound over their menfolk to labour at the city.

The work continued faster than ever after the newcomers arrived and they helped complete a large hut for the Eldest, divided by a partition into two rooms with floors made from a trodden mixture of clay and straw. They plastered the inner walls with mud for coolness in summer and warmth in the winter months. Besides other, similar dwellings for the Kindred advisers who sat in council with Kayin, a mass of smaller huts began springing up at random within the encircling walls, despite Kayin's efforts to maintain an orderly pattern of thoroughfares and open spaces. The new clan did not keep to separate quarters for men and women, and each family group hurried to claim a patch of ground. Even the smallest children busied themselves in brick-making for their new home. As the level ground became a warren of winding alleys connecting cramped, single-roomed houses, Kayin was at first angry, seeing how little they differed from the old village huts. Then he shook his head with a wry smile. The people would learn. He would teach them the beauty he had glimpsed in his dream.

After many hours in council, he decreed that the Kindred would move from the village at the start of the winter rains. Although the city would not yet be finished, the surrounding land could already be ploughed up for planting. The soil there was richer than the old village fields and Kayin anticipated a fine harvest. He ordered the people to build clay bins for storing the surplus grain. His advisers publicly praised his wisdom, and Kayin triumphed in the thought that he could at least command others to till the earth, even if he dared not do so himself. Whenever anyone raised their voice in fear or protest at leaving the sacred resting-place of the Kindred fathers, he would patiently explain his plan one more time.

'You must see,' he would say to the stubborn grandmother or troubled young man, 'that although I am Eldest, I am giving your hearts free choice. Those who wish to stay where they were born and reared can do so, and some will always remain to tend the tombs of our fathers. Can you not see that in this way the fathers receive even more honour? It is as if the whole village is consecrated to them as sacred ground and we will return from time to time to make thanksgiving offerings.'

At last Kayin decided that the city was ready to receive its people, even though not every wall was finished and some houses were still roofless. He gave orders that the Kindred would make their journey when five more days had passed, giving them time to gather their belongings and say farewell to those staying behind.

On the day of departure itself, soon after first light, he assembled the whole village to watch him pour jars of oil and fresh milk on the mound of Abu's grave and say a long prayer beseeching the fathers' goodwill—actions he saw as tiresome but necessary because of the people's superstitions. Not long afterwards, the huge cavalcade set off for their new home.

When they came in sight of the city walls, the men who had been left to guard the gateway gave a shout of welcome. For a moment, Kayin had a fleeting memory of his dream, but then he heard the silent streets filling with a babble of animal and human voices, and saw the ground churned up by hooves and strewn with fresh dung. The air throbbed with the sudden outburst of human life on what had once been an empty plain.

The city still had no name, although Kayin remembered the vow he made to his wife when he first heard about their unborn child. Only a few days after the Kindred's arrival, he went to the women's quarters to visit her and found a crowd of women barring the door against him.

'Nena's time has come,' said one. 'You cannot see her until the child is delivered.'

'But so soon?' Kayin was taken aback. 'She said it would be at the ending of the rains and there are still many days to go.'

The woman shrugged. 'You are a man. You know nothing of these matters.'

So soon, said Kayin to himself. His heart pounded. Would he really see his child with his own eyes? Was there really a child at all? Suddenly his mind was crowded with fears. Would the child be scarred? Twisted? Would it live? If he, Kayin, could not plant a grain of wheat without it shrivelling and dying, how could he hope to father another human life?

He rubbed the puckered skin on the side of his face, fingering the familiar lines. How could he not pass the blight to his innocent child? And how would it show itself? Would he see the stain of guilt in the eyes of the new-born baby or would it work its way out slowly, like a maggot burrowing up into daylight?

All the rest of that day and far into the night, he paced the streets of the city, returning again and again to stand by the hut where Nena laboured. Biting his knuckles, he thought of El for the first time in many days. Rage swelled in his throat.

'Thou shalt not!' he groaned at the night sky. 'Thou shalt not touch an innocent, helpless child!' *Even though I laid violent hands on my innocent brother, no wiser than a little child,* he thought—and flinched from the thought as from a touch on an open sore.

At a vague hour between midnight and dawn, Kayin came to the women's hut and found the door open to him. Drunk with weariness, he entered the room where they said his wife lay. He stood with his eyes lowered, terrified of what he might see, not daring to ask what had happened. Then he heard the smile in her voice.

'Come closer, my husband. Come and see your son.'

'My son?' he whispered.

'A fine, strong son!'

Kayin raised his eyes and saw the bundle Nena held in her arms. He thought of stretching out his hand to touch it, but suddenly hesitated. Perhaps the blight lay in his fingertips. Perhaps the child would be struck down even as he caressed it.

Nena laughed softly. 'Do not be afraid. You will not hurt him! I tell you, he is strong!' She seized Kayin's hand and placed it on the baby's warm brow. 'See how small he is, yet how strongly the life beats in him.' Kayin let his finger rest on the smooth skin, marvelling at his son's wise, wide-eyed gaze.

'He is beautiful,' he said huskily. 'And it is here—a city for our son, as I promised. All is well.'

In the morning, he presented the child to the Kindred, holding him up to the gaze of the assembled crowd at the city gates.

'Behold Kanoch!' he shouted, and the people cheered.

'The one who will be Eldest after me; the one for whom this city is named. I proclaim this place Kanoch, home of the Kindred, strongest tribe of the plains!' The crowds cheered louder. The rest of the day was given over to a riot of dancing and feasting.

When Kanoch was six days old, Kayin took him back to the village, to Seriah's dark, dirty hut, in accordance with an ancient tradition of the Kindred. Every first-born son received a special blessing from the wise woman of the village and Seriah proudly continued the task which had belonged to the women of her family for forgotten years. She hobbled out to meet Kayin, grumbling under her breath, but she smiled an unexpectedly sweet smile when she saw the fat little fists of the baby waving in the air. She held Kanoch tightly, rocking him and mumbling endearments, and Kayin followed them both into the hut.

For a long while Seriah sat in silence, cradling the child in her lap, and eventually Kayin grew impatient and asked whether she was going to bless the child or not.

She seemed to wake from a dream. 'What name have you given him?'

'Kanoch. I told you so already.'

She nodded slowly, staring down at the child who had fallen asleep in the warmth of her arms. 'Kanoch. He will be the lord of the city that bears his name.'

'Well?' Kayin prompted. 'And how old will he be when I lie with the Kindred fathers? Will he have a prosperous life?'

An obscure look appeared on Seriah's face. 'You? You will not lie with the Kindred fathers.'

'What do you mean?' Kayin leaned forward. 'Explain your words!'

Seriah shook her head. 'I do not understand the pictures that come to me. You have often puzzled me, Eldest, as I try to see what lies before you.' She started to tremble. 'It frightens me, what I think I see. There is a doom upon you. You will wander and not find rest; always staying a while and then leaving. I try to see more but it is like a cloud, a white cloud that swallows the way ahead.'

'Can you...' Kayin swallowed, 'can you see anything more? Anything at all?'

'I do not know. The cloud hides what is to come. It frightens me.' As the old woman's voice rose to a wail, the baby woke and began to cry.

Disguising his fear with a show of anger, Kayin told her roughly to bless the child and she sobbed out a few words before thrusting Kanoch back at his father. Kayin backed away from the hut where she sat swaying backwards and forwards, moaning to herself. Clutching the baby tightly, he tried to check his own weeping, but before long he began running, the tears cold on his cheeks. He did not stop until he was back at the city gates where Nena was anxiously awaiting their return.

When she saw Kayin she gasped, 'My husband, what has happened? Did she refuse a blessing?'

Kayin struggled for calm. 'She blessed him. All—all is well.'

'But why...'

He checked Nena's questions. 'I think the child is hungry and I—I am tired. Leave me now.' Perplexed, she set off homewards and he watched her go. For the rest of the day he sat at the gates, watching the people passing by—his people who honoured him and greeted him with a bow, whispering to one another about his wisdom and foresight. But as he sat there, fear gnawed at him; fear that the curse still hung over him, allowing him a little freedom, if only to make the pain worse when the inevitable blow fell. Again and again he tried to tell himself that old Seriah was wrong, that her visions were often confused, but he did not believe his own reassurances. There was something, there was still something waiting for him in future time. But he had to forget about it. He had to put it out of his head, or the thought would drive him mad.

Day followed day and Kayin anxiously watched his son, dreading the morning when he suddenly sickened or ceased to thrive. Kanoch, however, remained unshadowed by his father's forebodings and obstinately grew into a strong and sturdy child. There was a powerful bond of love between father and son, and as soon as Kanoch was old enough to stagger around, Kayin took him into the city streets, showing him the inheritance which would one day be his. Men and women smiled and clapped their hands when they saw the Eldest and his heir walking together.

When nearly two years had passed since the foundation of the city, a small clan of nomads came one day to discuss trade terms with Kayin. They proposed favourable rates for exchanging the thick fleeces of their flocks for the fine clay pots made by the Kindred, with the allowance that they could settle on some of the city grazing land during the coming winter. When the bargaining was over, the clan chief broke bread with Kayin who told him a little of how the Kindred had come to settle in their newly-established home.

'My grandfather once saw a marvellous sight in the hill country far to the south-east of your city,' the chief remarked. 'You say the Kindred are numerous, but the tribe he saw in those hills almost outnumbered your people. They were gathered for the burying of a man and a woman so aged that nobody remembered how long they had lived. My grandfather said they were the very founders of the tribe, but that I cannot believe. He always told how a man grown old and bent-backed himself stood and grieved over the bodies before they were put in the ground. The tribe did not worship their fathers but a spirit they called El, and the old man cried aloud to the spirit to have mercy on his dead father and mother who had suffered grievously. My grandfather always told how the pain in the old man's voice made even him, a stranger, weep. It seems there had been two older sons who had disappeared in the blossoming of their youth, and even the coming of the third son never healed the hurt of that loss.'

Kayin made no reply, all speech taken from him by the tale. Even as he tried to deny the idea, he knew with increasing certainty that it told of his father and mother. They were gone, but before they died they had had another child. He had another younger brother. The story even spoke of El—and Kayin shuddered as he said the name in his heart. But it was strange, so strange, that this chief should speak of what his grandfather saw; of something that had happened in the far past. And even then Kayin's new, younger brother was an old man. He felt so dazed by what he had heard that he could not grieve at the news of the death. Suddenly and desperately, he wanted to share the news with somebody and talk over the tale, but the Kindred believed that his family had died in a storm not long before Kayin came to them. How could he reveal the truth now?

Saying an abrupt farewell to the clan chief, Kayin left the hut and walked restlessly through the twilit city with some thought of finding Ani, his first friend among the

Kindred. As he passed his wife's quarters, he decided to pause long enough to swing Kanoch in his arms if he were not already sleeping. Stepping through the doorway, he could hear his wife's voice in the inner chamber, singing a lullaby to the child. The hut was otherwise deserted and, on an impulse, Kayin made his way to where she sat by the child, her black hair hanging down like a shining curtain. His shadow loomed vast against the wall as he crossed in front of the oil lamp burning steadily in its corner niche.

'Will he wake if we speak softly?' he whispered.

'You wish to speak with me?' Nena looked at him timidly.

'Do not always be so fearful!' Kayin said impatiently and watched her flinch from him. Awkwardly, he took her hand in his. 'Let us be companions as well as man and wife. Come outside with me and talk.'

She followed him out and stood before him, head bowed. He hesitated, wondering whether he could possibly unburden himself to her. 'Nena, you are part of the Kindred in a way that I could never be. Tell me your lineage. Tell me about your family; how you are so rooted in your people that you could not flourish away from them.'

Dutifully, she began recounting her ancestry, generation by generation, reaching back in a list of names to the first father and mother of the Kindred. When she had finished, she waited expectantly for Kayin to speak again.

At last he opened his mouth, unable to bear the torture of keeping secrets any longer. 'Will you hear my story? Of how I was lost from my kin?'

'In a storm, you said. They died before you came to...'

He interrupted fiercely, 'You have not heard the whole

story. None of the Kindred ever heard it—not even Abu. If you will listen, I shall tell you, because you are my wife and because I must trust somebody with it.' She nodded dumbly and he began. The darkness thickened around them until her listening face was an indistinct blur against the wall of the hut.

11
Retribution

When Kayin had told the whole of his story, omitting not a single part from the first days of the garden on the plateau to his arrival at the village of the Kindred, Nena was motionless; a pale statue at his side. He touched her shoulder and she stifled a cry. Even in that brief touch he could feel that she was shaking.

'Nena...' he tried to speak soothingly. 'Nena, my heart is lighter because I have told you.'

She answered in a voice as small as the singing of a gnat. 'As you will, my husband.'

'And you are willing to share this secret with me?'

'Whatever my husband wishes.'

'Go and sleep then.' He embraced her clumsily. 'We will talk further in the morning.'

She retreated without turning her back on him, and he waited for a moment to see if she would emerge from the hut again, thinking him gone and running to spill his secret to her companions. But she did not. He walked back to his hut and sank into a heavy slumber as soon as he laid himself on his mat.

Waking early the next morning, he felt unexpectedly enveloped in a sense of well-being. His secret was not hidden any longer. In that single act of telling, he had broken the loneliness which cut him off from other men and women, and he knew he should be afraid at his own daring. Instead he felt rested, emptied of harrowing emotions. *Soon,* he said to himself, *I will fear nothing and the curse will be broken. I will reach out in love to all people.* And he lay at peace, watching a dung-beatle trundling its ball of eggs across an interminable expanse of hard-packed earth.

Some time later, he was surprised to hear muffled voices outside the hut: three, maybe four men in anxious debate. When they called if they might enter, he could not rouse himself to reply, wanting to lie a while longer in restful peace. Eventually their footsteps shuffled cautiously into the outer chamber.

'Perhaps he still sleeps,' said one and Kayin recognised the gruff tones of Nena's father, Du. Then they caught sight of him through the doorway, lying on his mat.

'Eldest...' Du began and stopped.

'What is your business?' Kayin asked as he got to his feet. The men lowered their eyes respectfully as he tied on his skirt and swept his hair out of his eyes. Then in a confused huddle they emerged before him and he saw, besides her father, Nena's older brothers—all three of them slack-jawed, low-browed and doggedly protective of their family's honour.

'What is your business?' he repeated, feeling a twinge of unease, and Du stepped forward, rubbing his hands together.

'You must know, Eldest,' he said, 'that my daughter—your wife—she is distressed. She returned to us in the night and what she has told us...'

Kayin saw their faces obscured by a blood-red fog of fear which rose to blind him. 'Go on.'

Du twisted his big hands. 'It is terrible, Eldest, what she has told us.'

One of his sons interrupted. 'She told us you killed your brother and that the story you gave to the Kindred was lies.' The four of them stared at him accusingly.

'What do you say, Eldest?' Du persisted. 'Such tales bring dishonour on us all, but my daughter swears you told her these things.'

Kayin could not meet their increasingly hostile gaze. Dizzy with panic, he clutched at stray words. 'It was not all lies.'

Suddenly one of the three brothers cried out in fury. 'It is true! You can see it in his eyes. He is a murderer and a liar, and he has dishonoured our family and our people as well!'

'What have you done?' said Du in a dreadful voice. 'What have you done, Eldest?' And at the sound and memory of those words, Kayin dropped to his knees, burying his face in his hands.

They grew bold then, demanding that he should accompany them before the council of advisers to make full answer to the charges so that justice could be done. Although they did not quite dare lay hands on him, they hustled him through the street to Kish's door. He did not resist, still dazed by what was happening.

Kish was at first incredulous when the accusers poured out their story.

He took Kayin's arm and led him aside from the others. 'They are calling for the judgement of the council, Eldest! What foolishness is this that has so deceived them? Send them away!'

Kayin turned his haggard face to him and saw that its

appearance startled him. 'No, summon the rest. It is too late to set the matter aside.'

'But, Eldest, surely it is all a nonsense?' Kish said with a touch of irritation. 'Surely there is no truth in it?'

'Call the council together,' said Kayin thickly. 'I will give full answer to the charges.'

While Kish sent messengers to the other advisers, Kayin stood apart, despair overtaking the fear inside him. *It is the curse,* he said to himself. *It made me disclose my secret and that disclosure brings ruin upon me. I cannot escape.* At the same time, he felt a kind of relief that he was no longer hiding his past, that he might now face punishment for his crime. No punishment, not even death, could be so terrible if it brought an end to the curse.

Then he thought of Kanoch, his helpless little son. What would he have to suffer because of his father's sin? Suddenly Kayin wanted to fight. He would deny every word of his accusers; have them beaten for spreading lies. Anything to stop the stain touching his innocent child.

But he had run out of time. As he turned to confront Du and his sons, the rest of the council were arriving at the door. By the black looks which some of them gave him, it was clear that Nena's story was spreading already. Calling them to attention, Kish brought Kayin to stand before them and once again Du gave his account of the charges against the Eldest. While he was still speaking, a young man burst in from the street without asking for entry.

'There is something more you should know,' he panted, ignoring the angry muttering at his disturbance. 'Whatever the Eldest has done in the past, he has wronged me. He stole the loyalty of my wife, given to me by her father, Abu.' Kayin recognised him as Kidu, Ani's husband, and could do nothing but listen as the young man continued. 'I know the Eldest can take as many wives as he chooses, but he cannot take what already belongs to another man. Ani will not bed with me and she thinks only of the Eldest and how she can please him. He deliberately set out to take her.'

'That is not true,' Kayin said, but nobody heard him. They had turned to the person who had quietly entered with Kidu—Abu's second son, come in triumph to claim his rights.

'I always knew that my father was deceived by this man you call Eldest,' the newcomer said. 'And now the Kindred will be shamed throughout the land because they took for their leader a lying, murdering vagabond. And the truth was only uncovered when he was foolish enough to boast of what he had done.'

The council was confounded. Kayin could hear their murmurings from where he stood. Such a trouble had never come upon the Kindred before. How could they discover the truth of the matter and save the honour of the people? The man who brought them to the city and made them a people of renown was proved a deceiver; someone who laid violent hands on his own flesh and blood and boasted about it afterwards.

Abu's son interrupted their debate. 'The council must act to purge us of our guilt in following this man, or disaster will visit us.' He paused, and with a shrewd glance around the crowded room he added, 'If we do not act, the fathers' rage will strike soon. I believe it has ripened in the years we served this man and when it comes upon us, it will be beyond imagining.'

He may not believe in the power of the fathers any more than I do, said Kayin in his heart, *but he can call upon it to bring the council cringing to his heels like dogs.*

'What answer do you make, Eldest?' Kish gestured to the others to stop talking as he addressed Kayin.

It was as if Kayin was struck dumb. As he groped for words, the silence in the room grew heavier.

'The charges I have heard...' he faltered eventually, and broke off as yet another intruder rushed through the door. Hair and clothing dishevelled, her face scratched and bleeding, Ani flung herself at his feet.

'Tell them it is not true,' she sobbed. 'Tell them it is evil gossip. You are a good man and they must believe you! I will not let them harm you.'

'This is evidence of what I told! What further proof do you need?' yelled Kidu, and the colour drained from Ani's cheeks as she heard his voice. The room filled with chaos, uproar. Ani was weeping and clutching at Kayin as her husband tried to pull her away. Abu's son called for justice for himself and a beating for his faithless sister. The council were arguing together, cursing one another, cursing Kayin, even cursing Kish as he tried to restore order.

He stepped close to Kayin. 'Who are you really? Where have you come from?'

'No more than a dead man now.' Kayin did not know what he was saying. 'I could not escape any longer.'

'So is the story true?' Kish gasped. 'How could the fathers have allowed such a thing to happen?'

'You want truth, you say?' Kayin abandoned restraint, spilling out his anguish. 'Listen, then. The fathers have no power over the living. They are simply dry bones buried in the dust. Your worship of them is worthless.'

Kish paled in horror. 'You cannot say such a thing! You are a blasphemer!' His shout drowned the rest of the tumult. 'Blasphemer! You cannot be Eldest and defy the fathers!' Snatching Kayin's staff of office from his hand, he snapped it across his knee.

After that they dragged him from the hut, hauling him through the streets to the city gates, gathering a mob as they went. Abu's son marched in front, crying that they had unmasked a wicked deceiver. As the story passed from mouth to mouth, Kayin saw, as if from a great height, that his people were believing it and turning against him, their faces twisting with hate. They were going to stone him with the very rocks they had brought for building the city, and in a detached way he wondered how it would feel when the first stone struck, and how long he would take to die. This time it would be his blood that soaked the ground.

When they came to the gates, almost all the Kindred were assembled there already. Kayin could see no sign of Nena, even though he searched for her among the crowd as Kish proclaimed the sentence of death and raised his hand for the stoning to begin.

'Wait! You cannot do this!'

People looked round in astonishment as the frail voice called out again. 'I tell you, you cannot do this!'

Old Seriah was fighting her way through the ranks of people. 'He is set apart!' Limping to Kayin's side, she shrilled at them all, 'You cannot kill him. He carries the mark of the fire which touched him, yet spared his life. I saw it in a dream.'

'But he has shamed and dishonoured our people!' Abu's son shouted back.

Seriah took no notice. 'We must spare him. In my dream I saw his dead body on the ground and the Kindred lying dead around him and our city in flames. I have run from the village to warn you. We must not take his life.' By now everybody was listening to her. 'In my dream I saw that he must leave the Kindred, go from the city and never return. It is the will of the fathers. I saw it last night as I dreamed, even the secret he carried.' She peered up at Kayin. 'Your way turns from the Kindred, Mighty One. May you find rest one day.'

In the hush that followed her words, Kish spoke. 'Go. Do as she says. Go and do not look back, or the wrath of the fathers will strike you down.' Every onlooker was still and only their eyes moved, following Kayin as he stepped away from them and set one foot before the other, moving towards the open gateway. At the last instant, as he was about to pass the threshold of the city, he heard a child's whimper and knew it was Kanoch. He looked back and there was Nena, struggling to silence the boy who was crying for his father.

'Give me my son!' He started shouldering his way towards his wife. 'If I must leave, he will come too.' He did not feel the kicks and blows on his body as he struggled to get closer. 'Let me at least say farewell to him!' Kanoch's wail became a scream as he and his mother were hurried away, and the crowd's pent-up hysteria broke loose. Hurling whatever their hands could find and baying till they were hoarse, they drove Kayin through the gates, across the fields and out into the wilderness.

12

The Wanderer

'So where did Kayin go after he left the Kindred?' I asked the old man.

He gazed past me to where the late afternoon sun shone through the doorway and touched the stone walls with yellow. 'Far, perhaps further than any man has ever travelled. And for longer too.' He spread his parchment hands vaguely. 'Understand, my son, that in that time of exile he began to understand how the curse went deeper than he could have imagined, and to see why it was that Seriah could not foretell his life's end. It was...a disconnection.'

'Disconnection?' I tried to fathom the pilgrim's words.

'For Kayin, time passed differently. He was cut off from the normal passing of years. That was why he saw the founders of the Kindred and thought only an hour had gone by when he returned and discovered a whole village. When he drew closer to the human world of small deeds and small lives, the days wore away one after another in the familiar pattern, but when he was driven back into the wilderness where no people walked, things changed.'

'You mean he was immortal?' I asked excitedly.

The old man looked at me with eyes like cold ashes. 'He was cursed. There is no joy in endless life if each breath and each heartbeat remind thee of thy helplessness. To live without hope of escape from thy doom is a terrible thing.'

I shivered. 'Forgive me, my Father. I spoke thoughtlessly. But where did Kayin go? Did he meet other people again? What roads did he follow?'

The pilgrim's black mood seemed to lift and he nodded, almost smiling. 'Remember that Kayin was journeying before the Deluge unmade and reshaped the lands. He went into places now lost or changed beyond recognition, living off wild fruits, hunting with a bow and stone-tipped arrows, roaming onwards. Although he stopped counting the days after he left the Kindred, he woke every morning in pain and grief because he had lost his son. Where he travelled, he saw no other humankind and sometimes he would weep salt tears as he walked, weeping until he was blind. But Brendan, thou shouldst know that when the human heart shrinks from others into coldness and emptiness, the living emotions wither. The time came when Kayin forgot love, keeping only a memory of it, and even forgot hate and bitterness. The time came when all he knew was the urge to survive, to find food and a safe place to sleep for the night. He became like a wild animal: restless, homeless and living by instinct.'

'Where did he go?' I asked.

'He went north first, keeping the rising sun on his right hand. He crossed icy mountains where his feet sank in deep snow and came to a forest where satyrs danced in the glades; their faces human, their hind parts the hairy, cloven-footed legs of goats. The people of that country worshipped the satyrs and left gifts of food for them, so Kayin stole the food and walked on to a cold, dark land where the men had skins as white as death and rode about on dogs the size of ponies. Then he grew tired of the coldness and the darkness and went east.

'As he walked east, the setting sun cast his shadow before him. He crossed two rivers so wide that he could not see the far shore and came to the edge of the desert country of the basilisk whose glance turned men to stone, poisoned the streams, split the rocks, burned the grass and turned the fruit black and rotten. Even the birds flying over that country died and fell on the bare earth. So Kayin skirted that place and went still further east to a land of high red hills where he saw wild asses with white coats and blue eyes, and each had a twisting horn springing from its brow. And as he went eastwards again, he came to the beginnings of paths and saw smoke in the distance and knew he must be nearing a country thronged with men and women. He had been so long in the empty lands that he was afraid to come among people, so he turned his face to the south.

'As he went south, the sun disappeared in mist and cloud, and he came to mountains brimming with fire and molten rock. He ventured as close as he dared, even though the heat blistered his face. He saw the tiny fire lizards, the salamanders, darting among white-hot flames. And he went further south and came at last to the shore of an ocean where sea monsters floated on the waves like islands, and dived and sank and surfaced, spouting water from their huge heads. He saw there a race of yellow-skinned people as tall as the tallest trees. They lived on nothing but fish, pounding it into paste to make bread, and building their huts from the bones.'

I laughed. 'Travellers always tell strange tales.'

The old man frowned. 'I speak only of what Kayin saw,

just as thou canst see me lying here. But Kayin's wanderings were one day brought to an end, although he could not say how long he had travelled—whether a few years or many lifetimes of men. It was the Deluge, catastrophe beyond human reckoning, that ended his journey.'

The stormclouds had been gathering for days, massing on every horizon, blotting out the sun and sky and turning the seas an ominous grey-green. Kayin noticed, too, that the birds had disappeared, leaving the shore empty and silent except for the fierce wind rasping the sands. Further off, he saw ranks of white-capped waves tumbling forward to break over the reefs guarding the bay where he stood. He feared storms and whenever he heard thunder and saw lightning whiplash across a black sky, he would run to hide like a frightened animal. The storm now brewing would be terrible indeed and the air crackled with tension. Kayin felt the lines of the old scar throb on his face, and his hands shook as he scooped up water to moisten his dry mouth.

The sea no longer daunted him as it had done when he first sighted it countless days ago. He had been wandering uncertainly along the coastal edge of the land, unsure which direction to take since he could no longer travel south without crossing the water. Watching the fishing people from a distance as they navigated the breakers in their absurd little coracles, he wondered whether he could build such a craft and set off on a new path. All the time, though, the storm was swelling in the sky, and one morning the fishing people vanished, leaving Kayin alone and still undecided.

Wiping the drops of water from his lips, he pressed his palms against his aching eyes. The light was failing early because of the heavy clouds and he had to find a place to sleep where he would be safe from the packs of wild dogs which hunted in the countryside at night. Eventually he settled himself in the fork of a fir tree, in a grove safely beyond the highest tide-line on the shore. As he drifted into sleep, he could feel the wind tossing the branches above him so that it sounded as if the murmur of the sea was all about him.

When his eyes opened on thick, roaring blackness, he thought at first that he was still dreaming. The tree was shaking so violently that he had to clutch at the ridged bark to stop himself falling. As he woke fully, he realised that the storm had come. A hurricane of wind and ice and rain was battering the wood, hurling whole branches through the air and bending and snapping trunks like twigs. Kayin's limbs were so numb with cold that he almost fell as he climbed to the ground.

For a few eerie seconds, lightning tore the darkness open, showing Kayin the terrible sea. The tide was still flowing and the onshore wind brought every mountainous wave closer to where he stood. Then darkness closed in again and the storm thundered, a sound like mountains crashing down into ruin. His teeth chattering and his body a spasm of shuddering, Kayin plunged back into the wood, heading for higher ground where he would be safe.

He hoped for dawn, but there was only a faint lifting of the gloom, a flicker of damp light, before the clouds grew even thicker and the torrents of rain became like a solid sheet of water gushing from the sky. Kayin huddled beneath a ridge of rock, watching the river below him rise higher and higher until it burst its banks, turning the valley into one vast turbulent lake. The rain fell harder, piercing Kayin with its cold touch and driving him from his shelter to climb into the hills, trying to keep a spark of warmth in his body. To his relief, the violent fire and thunder of the storm had stopped, although the rain still fell and the hurricane drove the sea inland, filling Kayin's footprints as he fled.

For three days he ran from the flood, climbing yet higher as the waters crept inexorably upwards. River after river overflowed and merged to form new lakes, while the sea surged further in, leaving no trace of the ravaged shore. Sometimes another thunderstorm rumbled on the horizon, but when it ceased, the rain continued. All Kayin could hear, night and day, was the downpour, water falling on water. Each raindrop deepened the ominous silence which was obliterating birdsong, animal cry, rustling leaf and the faint stir of human activity.

On the fourth morning, Kayin realised that the flood was rising faster than he could travel. Although he struggled on with as little rest as he could bear, he could see already that the hilly ground of that country would not be high enough to escape the hungry tides. If the waters continued to rise, his remaining hope of survival was to build a craft like the coracles of the fishing people. Finding a cluster of oak saplings on one of the slopes, he set about lashing together the pliable boughs, stuffing the cracks with handfuls of sodden grass and leaves to make it as waterproof as he could. A churning, mud-brown torrent flowed yards from where he worked and the rain fell as hard as ever, but he took no notice, confident that the weather must surely change in a day or so. Meanwhile he would fashion just such a paddle as the fishing people had used and steer his coracle over the flood.

By the following noon he had finished his work and the small vessel was ready for launching. Heaving it to the water's edge, he pushed it cautiously into mid-stream. The current was stronger than he realised, pulling at the coracle as he tried to control it with the roughly-shaped wooden paddle. Sweating in spite of the cold, he recalled the deft manoeuvres of the fishing people who had floated over the waves like flakes of foam. Wielding the paddle, he attempted to steer a course as the current carried him swiftly inland, flowing with the tide from the distant ocean.

Suddenly a new, angry sound shook the air, a roar like a hundred lions stalking prey together. Kayin looked up and saw rushing towards him a towering, tawny-brown wall of water, sweeping down between the hills and topping the swollen tidal stream. There was no time to think of escape and he took a deep breath, clinging with all his strength to the frail boat as the wave descended. The coracle overturned, but he managed to clutch at it so that the waves did not drive them apart. Gasping and spluttering, he somehow kept his head above water as the wave dragged him towards the sea.

He drifted helplessly on the deep from then on. Although he righted the coracle, he could do nothing else because he had lost the paddle and there was no sign of land in any direction. Tasting the water, he found it brackish, unpleasantly tainted with salt, but still drinkable. Perhaps he had not yet come as far as the open sea. He could not tell.

Occasionally he saw dead creatures floating past—a buffalo, an antelope, a panther, even men and women—all bloated and disfigured. Sometimes he saw animals so huge, so monstrous, that they frightened him even in death with their enormous upturned bellies, their snake-like necks, the armoured bodies, the flipper feet as broad as he was high. The eddies of the flood carried them by and he watched until they drifted out of sight.

At first a terrible hunger gnawed at him and he tore at the raw dead flesh of any creature floating near enough for him to reach, but after a while he was too weak to do anything except lie gazing up at the rain pouring down out of the leaden sky. He huddled in the coracle, his body so chilled that he no longer felt pangs of hunger or thirst. He wondered if he was actually dying. The thought did not trouble him. His spirit was slowly cutting loose from his ravaged body and sometimes he felt himself rising high above it, gazing down at the little boat and the soaking heap of rags sprawled across it, calloused feet dangling in the water. Soon he would be gone too far away to care.

After a long time, he sensed something troubling him from a very great distance. Some slight matter had begun to clamour for notice. Gradually he returned to his senses and felt how painfully the splintered floor of the coracle cut into his skin and bone. He was no longer floating.

Moving slightly and groaning as his stiff joints unlocked, he realised that the boat had grounded. Another more startling realisation jolted him completely awake. The rain had stopped.

Before he could move again, something warm touched his forehead. His vision cleared and focused itself on the brown circles which floated above him. After a while, he realised that they were human faces, and above them he saw the pale, tremulous blue of a clear morning sky.

13

A High Place

The timid marsh-dwellers who found Kayin carried him and his battered coracle back to their reed huts in a clearing by a shallow lake. At first he was so ill and weak that he could only lie still on his rush mat watching the sunlight filtering through the gaps in the woven walls, but they nursed him, giving him water to drink and a soft, tasteless stew of fish and lentils to eat. Eventually he was able to leave his bed and sit for a while in the leafy shade of a palm tree.

His rescuers fished for their food guiding their high-prowed boats along the meandering river channels of that delta-country. They laughed at his coracle, refusing to believe that he ever saw people sea-fishing in such a craft. When they questioned him about his past life, touching his scarred face wonderingly, he pieced together an account of the flood and a memory of his time with the Kindred. He told them that he had lost his tribe in the terrible Deluge. They stared at him blankly.

'Deluge? Days of rain? A lake as wide as the open sea?' laughed one of the young men. The marsh-dwellers' speech was not unlike the Kindred's, although most of their talk and many of their words were concerned with boats, fishing nets, the thickness of sea-mist and the teeming varieties of biting fly and mosquito which infested the marshes. 'We have rains in winter, yes, and the rivers sometimes flood, but your illness must have given you bad dreams. A lake like the open sea!' The others joined in his laughter, but it was not cruelly mocking laughter because they were kindly people.

'Surely you saw it too!' Kayin persisted. 'When you first found me, the sky was only just clearing after the storms and you told me you were glad the rains had finished.'

His listeners frowned at one another and Kayin saw, too late, the trap into which he had fallen. The passage of years had somehow dislocated in the storm, leaving him stranded once again in a foreign place and time. But how could he explain that to these simple marsh-dwellers?

Suddenly one of the older men quietened the others and addressed Kayin. 'I heard tell of a great flood once.'

'When?' Kayin caught his breath.

'Many, many years ago, in the time of our grandfathers' grandfathers. The story tells how the rains fell and made waters so deep that they almost swept the world away. Maybe you heard the story once and dreamed as you lay ill with fever from the winter rains.'

'Maybe.' Kayin hung his head. He was cut off from all other living men, a ghost from the half-forgotten past.

Finding himself among men and women again, he felt unexpected, long-buried emotions returning—resentment, disillusion and, above all, a deep sense of betrayal. He remembered with sharp clarity how the Kindred, how his wife, had cast him out, although he had given them a city and greater renown than they had ever dreamed. Why should even the gentle marsh-people prove different? He would not trust them. But beneath the hard anger and resolve, he kept a faint memory of grief for Kanoch whom he had left back in the past and would now never see again.

He stayed on at the village of reed huts, even when he was strong enough to go back to his life of wandering, because he did not know what to do. He did not want to stay in the dreary swampland for ever, but where could he go? For the time being, it was easier to take advantage of the fishermen's freely-given hospitality. They demanded no return for their gifts of food, clothing and shelter. The women were more timid than their menfolk and rarely spoke to Kayin, but one day he tried to question one of the grey-haired grandmothers who had watched over him during his illness.

'Why did you bring me here? Why did you not leave me to die?' he asked, sitting cross-legged beside her as she stirred a pot of lentil porridge.

She looked at him with kindly eyes. 'You were sick and helpless, like a lost child. We had pity.'

Pity. Kayin found himself hating their pitying glances, thinking him a poor madman, deluded by his own wild tales. As he regained his strength, he grew impatient with their childish laughter and their simple ways. He began to feel that he could not stay there many days longer.

The time of his leaving was settled for him, however. One night he lay on his mat and heard voices outside in earnest discussion. Catching his own name among the muttered words, he crept to the doorway to listen further, but the circle of figures caught sight of him and quickly scattered.

Early next morning, three of the younger men came to him with an air of importance. They always spoke to

Kayin as equals and he realised he must have aged little in outward appearance since his first encounter with the Kindred.

'We have found your lost people,' they announced, grinning broadly. Kayin's jaw dropped. Surely they were mistaken. 'All this time you have stayed with us while your own people were camped nearby. Come, we will take you. You must go back to them.' Ignoring Kayin's protests, they took his arms and almost dragged him to a waiting boat. They were confident that they had solved the mystery of Kayin's past, and wanted the delight of watching the reunion with his people.

They paddled swiftly past reed thickets and groves of palm trees, startling a wild boar that had strayed from its herd to drink at the river's edge. As they went, Kayin wondered whether to throw himself into the water to try to escape from the ridiculous, mistaken circumstance. Then he looked at the strong shoulders of the fishermen and he knew they would be only too eager to rescue him. They thought they were taking him home.

The river looped and looped again until they were almost doubling back towards the village. Another slow bend unwound ahead and Kayin raised his head wearily as they rounded it, expecting another long vista of brown water bordered by dense groves of trees. Instead the land broadened out into a plain with a glimmer of dark blue mountains on the furthest horizon.

One of the young fishermen nudged Kayin and pointed excitedly. 'Look! They are here still, your people. See, their camp!' His heart beating hard, Kayin followed the other's pointing finger and saw five or six low black tents pitched near the riverbank. A straggling herd of goats grazed the rich grass and a small girl stood nearby, a peeled stick in her hand. When the boat drew alongside her, she ran to the tents and soon the bank was lined with silent men and women watching the newcomers suspiciously. Weak with relief, Kayin opened his mouth to tell the marsh-dwellers that they were mistaken, that these were not his people, but the fishermen were already calling cheerful greetings to the waiting crowd.

'Here he is—your chief. We found him and brought him back!' Kayin felt all the eyes turn on him. The fishermen were busy mooring the boat and climbing the sloping bank, but as they hauled Kayin up, one of the watching men moved to bar their way.

'He is not one of us. He has a strange face.'

The fishermen were certain that they were right. 'We are the ones who met you hunting near our village and you told us your chief was lost, and then we knew who it was we had found, almost dead, many days ago. We have brought him back to you.' Smiling uncomprehendingly at the man's protests, they scrambled back into their boat and glided away, shouting a last farewell to Kayin. He said nothing as they disappeared, feeling an obscure sense of relief that he had escaped their relentless kindness. He could easily walk away from these new, sullen people.

Realising he had not eaten that morning, he addressed the nearest woman coolly. 'Will you not offer me refreshment now that I am your guest?' Flustered, the woman nodded and beckoned Kayin to one of the tents. The rest of the tribe followed, jostling one another to get a better look at him and his scar. As he rested on a heap of cured goatskins, his audience gradually relaxed. They came closer and finally sat down around him, watching intently as he drank soured milk. The men whispered together and soon grew bold enough to speak to Kayin. He answered their questions about himself as briefly as he could, giving them the same story as he had the fishermen, and then contrived to turn the talk to themselves.

They were a broken-spirited little tribe who roamed the river plains with their flocks and a few tired pack-donkeys. Twelve days ago, while they were hunting wild boar in the marshes, the mists came down suddenly and their chief had been lost. Since then they had stayed camped in the same place, quarrelling about what they should do.

'And we do not know where to go,' said one man whose mane of curly black hair covered half his face. 'Some think we ought to wait till Eber, our chief, comes back, but others think we should go and find new pasture for the flocks.'

An older man sighed, lifting the twisted stump that was his right hand. 'I think we are under a curse. Five of our strongest youths, my son with them, were drowned in floods last spring. Enlil is always angry with us.'

Enlil? Kayin thought, and laughed inwardly. Perhaps there were indeed other gods besides the vengeful spirit he knew; gods who delighted in seeing men squirm miserably in the dust. Looking at the wretched, downtrodden people, their eyes fixed longingly on the baked fish the woman gave to him, he despised them in his heart. He was homeless, they were leaderless. The food tasted good and the women were not unpleasing. It would be easy to take power and rule them as he pleased.

'I will be your chief now,' he said aloud and sneered as the faces around him gawped stupidly.

He discovered them to be no more than twenty in number and poverty-stricken in spirit, although some of their possessions were far finer than anything the Kindred had owned. They used bronze axeheads which gleamed like morning sun on the river and they had so many clay cooking pots that they let the babies break them in play. Despite this wealth, they never held their heads proudly like the Kindred had done, and their cooking pots were squat and unlovely, marked with clumsily scratched decoration no better than a child's scribble.

He told them that they would journey north and he drove them onwards each day until the women and children cried with exhaustion. Kayin himself was still too weak to walk far and he rode at the head of the cavalcade on one of the donkeys. The brief spring was almost over and the dust rose in clouds from the dry earth as the people walked. As they travelled up-country, the north-eastern mountains drew closer each day and Kayin studied them for hours as he jogged along on the donkey's back. Something about their outline was familiar, like an elusive dream-memory, and suddenly he knew them, even though their silhouettes were blurred and changed in some way. They were the mountains where he had once lived with his father, mother and brother in the cave on the plateau.

Pulling on the rope halter, he brought the donkey skidding to a standstill. Just for a moment he allowed himself to wonder whether the unburied bones of his brother still lay whitening on a hillside or whether the waves of the Deluge had tumbled them to the bottom of the ocean. And now he, Kayin, maker of gardens, planter of cities, roamed the plains in a different age, governing a mean-spirited tribe, as graceless as their pack-animals. Fury at his fate surged inside him and he wrenched angrily at the halter of his donkey, goading it into a trot.

Later, as he slept under the night sky, he dreamed of a great city again for the first time since the building of the

Kindred's new home. He saw the tall gates opening for him as he walked alone up the hill, but the wide street had become a river and almond trees blossomed pink beside the clear water. When he awoke, he wept, hiding his tears in the long hair of the girl whom he had chosen for that night. Staring sleeplessly through the entrance of the tent, he imagined towers rising against the stars. A tower. A tiny seed of an idea took root in his mind, sending out tentative shoots, and he lay thinking until dawn reddened the sky.

They trudged on across the plains as the summer heat scorched their heads and Kayin tried to recall his journey of countless years before. This time, the land was thronged with inhabitants. Almost every day they passed a settlement, sometimes no more than three flimsy huts with an encircling mud wall to keep out enemies. Sometimes it was a bustling village built up on a platform because of the annual floods. Kayin saw nothing as fine as the city of Kanoch. He wondered if it still stood somewhere, but the new world through which he walked was so bewildering that it almost drove out the memories of the past. Yoked teams of oxen dragged wooden ploughs through the earth which was irrigated by ditches brimming with river water. After fording another river, they came to places still more crowded with small villages where men stopped their work to stare at the travellers. The people looked well-fed and comfortable and were often reluctant to exchange measures of grain for one of the tribe's skinny young goats.

Meanwhile Kayin was honing his plan. First, a tower like a mountain peak, higher than any other work of man—the craftsman's dream renewed after the years of hardship and exile. A tower built by the tribe to draw others who would sit at his feet to hear his vision and then offer their labour to build the city; a city even greater than in the days of the Kindred.

When he finally revealed his dream to the tribe, he won their agreement by playing on their fears of the strange gods they served. During their nomad life they had pieced together bits and scraps of many beliefs, chiefly revering Enlil, Lord of storms, who brought floods to punish the disobedient. Worse than Enlil were the malevolent spirits, the demons lurking in the river, the air and the night shadows.

'We will build a high place,' he told them. 'A place reaching the stars where men can speak to the gods face to face above the dust of everyday life. The gods will respect your proud spirit and you will no longer live in fear of them. Besides that, we will show our strength to the people hereabouts and they will submit to us.' Easily persuaded by his eloquence, the tribe accepted every word and pledged loyalty to him with fumbling eagerness. To show his authority over them, he marched them mercilessly for nearly a week until they came to a large expanse of empty land. Ordering them to make camp, he rode around to survey the site, satisfying himself that the ground was sufficiently level and firm. Returning, he called for the tribe's attention.

'We will build it here,' he said. 'Tomorrow you will start making bricks.'

14

Tongues of Flame

The people sweated in the hot sun, their arms and faces caked with mud. Kayin paced among them, surveying their bent backs with satisfaction. The work went faster than he had dared to hope, and round each deep clay-pit stood a pyramid of dried bricks. Nearby lay the rows of wooden moulds, so large that it took two men to lift each one, and on the other side of the camp were the kiln-fires baking bricks for the strong outer skin which would keep the tower from crumbling. Kayin watched one girl, only ten years old, kneeling beside her mother and helping to pack one of the moulds with fistfuls of clay. A group of boys were stamping round in a circle by the pits, treading a mixture of mud and chopped straw with their bare feet. Even the youngest children were busy carrying dung to fuel the fires and bringing water for their thirsty parents.

The usual cluster of onlookers watched the activity from a careful distance and when Kayin approached, one woman called out to him, asking what they were doing. He told her and she rolled her eyes disbelievingly at her companions. Wheeling round, he stalked back to where his people laboured and began pacing among them again, urging them to work faster. Behind him the onlookers were laughing.

'A tower touching the clouds!' jeered the woman who had spoken to him. Kayin gritted his teeth. *They will be sorry they laughed*, he told himself, *when I am lord of this land. Then they will come crawling to me begging for mercy.*

Walking beyond the camp towards the river, he came to the place where building would soon commence. He had measured out the site before they had made the first brick mould—120 paces long, 200 paces wide. In his mind's eye he could see the tower clearly, seven terraces rising one above the other, each diminishing in area and yet taller than the one below. A mountain of bricks, with even the first terrace standing twice the height of a man, and a stairway built into the side so that one day he could climb to the top and see his city spread out beneath him.

A shout came from the clay-pits. 'Call the chieftain! They are coming and the donkeys are heavy-laden!' It must be the return of the three men whom Kayin had sent westward with all the pack-animals he could spare to bring the first of many loads of bitumen—the black tarry substance which they would use as mortar. Hurrying back to meet them, his heart sang with excitement. Now they could lay the first bricks for the base of the tower.

As the next weeks passed, the outlines of the first terrace took shape and the groups of watchers became crowds. Kayin took care to plant rumours among them so that they went away telling one another that the grim chieftain with the scarred face was building a home for the gods, and that he had spoken to them in a dream, and that his scar was their mark upon him. He saw fear and awe on men's faces as he went by, and no one questioned his authority. While most of the crowds returned to their own villages after a day or so, others lingered and a few asked permission to join Kayin's people. When the harvest was over, more came, and by the summer Kayin saw that his plan for adding to the labourers had been successful, just as in the days when the Kindred built their city.

One night he was dragged from sleep by shouts and the sounds of a scuffle. Five strangers had been caught trying to break down a newly-built wall. When they were brought in front of Kayin, they refused to speak until he threatened to hand them over to the furious tribe. Then they confessed that they were sent by the chief of the nearest village who was jealous of Kayin's growing renown among the people thereabouts. Kayin let them go after binding them to work for him from the very next morning, but he commanded his tribe to set a guard on the tower.

Each evening as darkness fell, the people lit a defensive ring of beacons around the camp and the men would gather together, easing tired muscles after the day's labour and talking quietly. Kayin overheard them sometimes—'May Enlil be merciful to us now...they say we will touch the sky-realm of Anu...I will climb the tower and make libations to Sin, Lord of the Diadem...the gods will be kind, as in the days of our fathers' fathers.' Kayin felt a surge of contempt for their foolish chatter. He had no need of gods. His god had turned his back on him and Kayin walked by himself.

The tower climbed higher into the heavens as the sun blazed out of a harsh blue sky. During the hottest hours, the labourers fanned themselves in the shade of makeshift tents and canopies, while clouds of flies whined in the dry air. People came from miles away to pledge loyalty to Kayin and he ordered some to return to their fields and bring tributes of food for the labourers and straw for the brick-making. Others he ordered to dig fresh clay-pits for when the old pits were exhausted. The rest joined the gangs on the tower. Summer ended and winter brought welcome coolness and even more men and women anxious to be part of the work.

From time to time someone would lose their footing on the terraces and fall. As the terraces rose higher, fewer escaped unharmed. Three men were carried groaning to their tents with broken bones when they fell one after the other from the third terrace. On two occasions men were killed. Kayin shuddered when he saw the blood on the ground and he gave leave for the victim's family to return home if they wished. Only one family did so, in the second winter when it rained for days and the bricks took as long as a week to harden.

As the third summer approached, Kayin sensed that the will of the people was weakening. They had toiled and struggled for so long, yet the tower was still incomplete. Some of the older men came to Kayin as he rested beneath a canopy one noon-time, asking when the work would be finished.

'When the last brick is placed on the last terrace,' he answered curtly. 'There are others to take your place if you are too tired to continue.'

'You promised us a city,' said one, blinking nervously, 'and homes for our children, but after two winters we are still camped here.'

'It is the people that we speak for,' added another whose darker skin showed that he came from the western desert. 'They are weary and they cannot believe the tower will stand seven terraces high as you tell us.'

'Very well,' Kayin said after a thoughtful pause. 'I will consider what you have said.'

Before the last of the men had stepped out into the heat, he knew what he would do and dispatched an attendant to spread the message from tent to tent. When the fifth terrace was finished, the people would have leave for a night of feasting and celebration, and the chieftain promised as much meat and drink as they wanted. Work on the tower would then resume, but there would be large rewards for those who stayed till the very end.

On the sixth day after his proclamation, Kayin left his tent as the afternoon sun shone level across the plains. Hearing the buzz of excitement as he approached the labourers, he smiled mockingly, thinking how easily he could win his way, buying men's allegiance with roast mutton and barleycakes. In the last six days, the fifth terrace had come within inches of completion. The tower threw a huge wedge of shadow over the ground and as Kayin stepped into the cool, he sensed the people's exuberance. The bricks passed from hand to hand with an easy rhythm, as if the feast harps were already playing, and people shouted and laughed when they had usually worked in silence. Kayin called for the foreman who came running down the tower stairway, beaming with anticipation.

'You come in good time, chieftain,' he panted. 'Climb up with me and you will see the last brick put in place.' He waved a hand at the busy site. 'We have worked without rest since daybreak.' Kayin followed him up the steep steps behind a young man who staggered under a heavy load of mortar. When they reached the top of the fifth terrace, he saw that work had stopped and the labourers stood awaiting his arrival.

'Come and see,' the foreman said eagerly. 'We have reached the end you set for us.'

Kayin stepped to the edge and looked down over the plains widening to the horizon, dotted with villages and divided by silver ribbons where rivers flowed. His domain one day.

'No,' he said abruptly. 'I do not care for ceremony. Put the last brick in place and go off to your feasting. I shall stay up here alone.'

Surprised, the foreman nodded assent and started shouting orders to his workers. Kayin heard, but did not acknowledge, the cheering which went up around the tower a few moments later as the last brick was stamped into place. Then bare feet scuffled past him to the stairway, and men jostled and joked as they hurried down to the camp. The sounds got fainter until Kayin was finally alone. The top of the tower offered no shade and the sky was still cruelly bright, so he drew his embroidered cloak over his head and sat down to watch the sun dipping towards the edge of the world.

Gradually light turned to twilight and the stars appeared, first singly and then by the score, until the whole night was blackness scattered with white jewels. From far below came a discordant blend of reed pipes, drumbeats and three-stringed harps. Riotous voices were half-drowned in fig wine. The beacon fires twinkled like sleepy red eyes and then the moon rose, blanching the darkness and turning the rivers on the ghostly plains to molten silver light.

Kayin found he had needed less and less sleep since his days with the Kindred, and he sat on the terrace for hour after long hour, gazing at the moon and imagining the straight streets of his city radiating out from the tower.

Although the night air was fresh, the breeze brought him the warmth from the sun-baked earth. When the breeze died and the moonlight faded, he stirred, thinking that dawn was coming sooner than he expected. The beacon fires were smaller and a darker red, and only a whisper of sound came from the camp from the last few revellers still awake.

Suddenly the air changed. It was no longer clear but stifling as if a storm was brewing, although no clouds hid the stars. The moon still shone above the horizon, but its light was dim, hiding the plains beneath confusing shadows. Kayin heard a rumble like thunder, remote yet surely coming closer. He scrambled to his feet, terrified that the storm might break while he sat exposed on the high tower. In the sudden obscurity, though, he could not be sure of his foothold and he dropped to his hands and knees, feeling his way towards the stairs.

Then he saw the shining mist. It passed so quickly that he only caught it with the tail of his eye. It was like a swarm of fireflies floating on the air currents. He could not tell where it came from. Leaning dangerously over the edge of the terrace, he saw the mist turning to darting lights, little tongues of flame flickering down over the camp. All at once they swirled together like a swarm of bees, and vanished as if someone had snuffed them out.

The wind blew cold through Kayin's cloak and the darkness was lifting on the eastern rim of the sky, so he set off down the steps, counting each one to keep his mind from the dizzy drop on one side. Had he dreamed the strange lights? On his return to the camp, he would find out whether anyone else had seen them. While he climbed, the sky turned from grey to pale grey, and then to an indeterminate colour. A pink line spread slowly in the east. Lower and lower, winding around the tower, the stairway brought him closer to the ground. For such an early hour, he could see an unusual amount of activity among the tents. Figures were swarming about like black ants, and soon he could hear a rising hubbub of noise.

A swollen red sun loomed in the dawn sky as Kayin took the last three steps in a single bound and entered a camp as frenzied as a trampled nest of scorpions.

'What is it?' he cried, holding up his hands to try to quell the uproar. Nobody answered him. They could not answer him. When they opened their mouths, they could form only a string of unintelligible sounds, not words. Kayin pushed his way through the howling mob, trying to reach the shelter of his tent where he could weigh up what was happening. As he moved forward, hands snatched at his cloak, bodies shoved against him so that he almost fell, and faces thrust against his own, mouths mumbling and shrieking an appalling gibberish. He realised that they were trying to talk to him, and that they were growing more and more panic-stricken as they could not even understand one another. Wrenching himself clear, he ran to his tent, knocking aside any who stood in his way. The foreman was waiting for him there.

'Chieftain!' he wailed, speaking, to Kayin's relief, in comprehensible words. 'It is a curse upon us. You have turned the gods against us!'

'I? I have done nothing...'

The other man interrupted him. 'You have brought the anger of the gods upon us with your tower reaching to heaven. It is madness! We woke from our feasting and our speech was changed to the cries of wild animals. Chieftain, what have you done?'

'I have done nothing,' Kayin shouted furiously. 'But you say it came in the night...'

'In the night,' the foreman interrupted. 'I saw nothing, but I woke and I was cut off from my own family. Their words have changed.'

Kayin remembered the bright cloud over the camp. What terrible thing had he brought upon these innocent people? A surge in the crowd outside the tent thrust a group of men inside, their eyes blazing with accusation.

'From the tower!' the foreman screamed. 'Throw him from the tower. He has angered the gods.' His gestures were clear enough for the other men to seize Kayin and start dragging him towards the foot of the stairway. Their fear had turned to a craze for some kind of revenge.

'It was his fault!' the foreman cried. 'This man with the scarred cheek, who spoke of meeting the gods between earth and heaven. It is he who has brought this disaster upon us!'

Kayin's fury was like ice in his blood and when he spoke, his voice cut through the tumult like a whetted knife.

'You will not touch me.' They did not know what he said, but at the sound of his voice their hands jerked away from him and hung awkwardly at their sides. 'You will not touch me. I am set apart.' The silence tingled and Kayin found that he was free to go. People shrank back, making a path for him as he strode to the border of the camp.

Turning to face them, he shouted, 'Your gods are nothing. This is the work of El. It is the curse I brought with me and I take it with me now.'

It seemed to him as he walked away that however many steps he took, however long he walked, he could not leave the tower behind. Whenever he looked back, he saw it rising tall in the morning air, growing ragged and misshapen as the labourers clawed at the bricks with maddened hands, pulling them down into ruin. Already some people were scattering, clutching their possessions in their arms, but none passed near him. He walked on alone.

When evening came, he could not see the tower any more. He waded into the shallows of a river which flowed broad and sluggish across the path he had been taking.

'I make my choice,' he said aloud, watching the water eddy around his feet. 'I will take my own life. I will make an ending.' He went forward so that the water rose to his knees, then his waist, then his chest. Then, closing his eyes, he went on deeper still.

PART TWO

'By Crist!' quod Conscience tho,
'I wol bicome a pilgrym,
And walken as wide as the world
lasteth...'

From *The Vision of Piers Plowman*
by William Langland

15

Under the Sun

'So Kayin died?' I could not believe that the old man's tale had ended so suddenly. Before his reply came, I heard footsteps approaching the cell and Ciaran, the brother next in age to me, entered with a frown on his face.

'A word with thee, Brendan,' he said, nodding a brief acknowledgement of the pilgrim. Following him outside, I was surprised to see that the sun had almost disappeared into the western sea. A kittiwake dipped and circled on the evening breeze. When it gave its mewing cry, the lonely sound wrenched at my heart after the story I had been hearing.

Ciaran led me away from the cells to where we would not be overheard. 'Brendan, where hast thou been? Thou didst not have leave to neglect all thy duties. I had to work the fields by myself today. If we go hungry next winter, it will be because of thy neglect!'

My temper rose at his rebuke. 'I have been doing a higher duty, Brother. The pilgrim has been making confession to me. I think he is dying.'

Ciaran folded his arms inside the wide sleeves of his habit. 'If I recall rightly, Brecan told thee to attend to his bodily needs and leave him to rest. And dost thou think thou art old enough to carry the weight of a man's confession?'

'But he says he has not long to live! He says he must tell the great tale he bears and then he will be free. It is too late for him to start telling it again to another.'

'This sounds like a strange matter,' Ciaran said, surprised. 'Hast thou told Brecan any of this?'

'When it is finished, I will tell it all,' I answered, adding virtuously, 'I will vow to fast and pray for him as he tells his story.'

Ciaran looked at me thoughtfully. 'I suppose it may be God's will for thee. I can see, Brendan, how thou dost warm people's hearts and draw them to thyself. I think sometimes that thou shouldst live in a wider world than this community.'

I interrupted Ciaran's musings. 'I will stay with him tonight. Couldst thou bring me a lamp to burn?'

Laughing, Ciaran pushed me back towards the pilgrim's cell. 'If thou must wait up, then do so by moonlight. I will not fetch and carry for thee.'

Returning to the old man, I sat in the deepening twilight as he talked on. For a while the darkness hid him from me but when the moon rose, its light spilled through the open doorway for a time, showing me the figure lying on the bed like a living statue.

Kayin did not die. He stood with the river water flowing around him and tried to throw himself under, but always at the last minute the will to live brought him to the surface for air. Eventually he waded back to the shore and hunched there, shivering. The thought came to him that perhaps he did not want to die, although he had nothing left: no family, no companions, no home. Yet his life still felt precious to him—and why should the curse of El drive him to destroy it? He resolved to stay alive.

So he took to journeying again, day after day, season after season, year after year, under the sun and under the moon. He renounced his dream of the city, and in his journeyings he saw other men's dreams taking form, for the world was changing. Men and women multiplied beyond belief and their clamour filled the empty lands, giving enduring names to the hills and valleys, the rivers and the plains. They shaped symbols on wet clay and papyrus and the symbols became words, and the words history, making the world a fixed, explicable place.

As the pilgrim's story flowed on like a quiet stream, I grew drowsy, and in my struggle to keep awake, I fell into a kind of waking dream. His words rang in my ears and I saw what the old man was describing as if I myself were Kayin the lonely wanderer.

I was walking on tireless limbs over the face of the earth, from nation to nation, through cities whose very names were the pride of men's hearts. Down the green ribbon of the Nile I journeyed, where the pharaoh's barges sailed in stately procession, and I stood among the temple colonnades at Thebes, praying to no gods. Near the eastern rim of the world I saw hundreds of men labouring to raise walls around their kingdom against the terrible demons of the wilderness. In the land of Shinar, kings sat in palaces of three hundred rooms, guarded by lions and bulls of alabaster, and I saw them feast on ostrich eggs and roasted grasshoppers. As I rested in palm-shaded courtyards, I watched slaves staggering to the banqueting halls with whole vats of wine. Among a crowd of a thousand I climbed the stairs of Persepolis to the audience hall where a great ruler awaited tribute from conquered peoples. In a desert country I passed through the glittering blue gates of Babylon, past the watchful dragons, and wept at the green splendour of the gardens where ferns spilled over the terraces and the liquid note of running water soothed the parched air.

I followed the traders' caravans, laden with cloth and aromatic oils, cold iron and silver, pungent spices and wretched humans taken into slavery. I came to the holy temple at Jerusalem, gleaming with gold and cedarwood, and then I stood on the shores of a calm sea thronged with sailing boats where wealthy merchants counted handfuls of coins. Taking ship, I came to an island of mountains where a labyrinthine palace stood, bright with frescoes and fearless young men and women who chanced death and leaped the charging bulls in the hot sunshine. Crossing the wine-dark sea again, I saw a hollow hillside where masked players moved in chorus, and a bay where a gigantic goddess of gold and ivory brooded over her city.

The empires stretched like webs across the lands and I saw them cut down and reformed as men fought against one another. I saw little kingdoms ruled by little red-faced kings with strident voices, dreaming of ruling great kingdoms and raising statues to their own magnificence. Assyrian, Babylonian, Persian, Greek, laying sieges and defeating strongholds, campaigning, rebelling, invading. And I was Kayin, and I felt sick at the blood spilled on the grass as soldiers butchered one another in battle, feeding enmity and hatred for generations. Robed priests lifted sacrificial knives in cruel ritual and slit the throats of snorting, trembling animals and even human prisoners, screaming for mercy as their lives were taken from them to please demon gods. Soothsayers consulted entrails, heaps of bones and the starry constellations, seeking good omens and trying to read the future.

Whole nations were carried away into exile and slavery while their homes lay destroyed behind them; the work of painters, sculptors and goldsmiths brought to ash and ruin. Warlords shackled captive princes to their chariots and drove them in shameful parade, and the humble people were trampled underfoot.

Above all, I saw that mankind lived in fear of death. Kings went to the grave with their children, their wives and even their servants who killed themselves to accompany their lord to the world of the dead. There were tombs everywhere, vaulted tombs like beehives where the dead were enthroned in mounds of precious metals, lapis lazuli and carnelian, but the humble people were buried in the dirt and their names were forgotten. Men toiled in vast quarries, driven by whips to build pyramids and funeral temples, and I followed a procession of priests and wailing women and a gilded coffin drawn on an ox-cart. But in the east I saw an emperor, dressed in his finest robe and brightest jewels, setting fire to himself in his own palace because his warriors had betrayed him and he feared death less than dishonour.

Then in the dream I returned in old pathways and found mighty cities brought to nothing. I came to Troy and it was in flames as an invading army ransacked the citadel, piling the jewelled necklaces, the bronze daggers and the silver goblets in the broken streets. I found Nineveh laid waste, pillars crumbling to dust and palaces decaying to hummocks of earth. The city walls of Babylon were destroyed and the temples razed, and I walked between mounds of rubble and wept again. Royal bones were scattered in the desert, and I found empty towns where the people had run away, going back to their old, squalid lives, forgetting the splendour of the cities and using the stones to build hovels. Some remembered and yearned for a lost golden age, but scarcely a trace remained of what had been.

There was a sour taste in my mouth and my bones ached. 'It is all worthless, all futile.' Were those Kayin's words or were they mine? The voice of the old pilgrim sounded in my head as I yawned into waking in the pale morning light—'Then Kayin came to Carthage, his heart burning within him.'

16

Sanctuary

The oarsmen in the bobbing tug-boat bent their backs and pulled hard so that the tow ropes rose taut and dripping from the water. Inching along, they brought the trading galley to its berth in the merchant harbour where the crowd waited on the quayside. Although Kayin stood apart from the excited crew who were already waving and shouting to old friends, he made himself follow their speech. During the long voyage along the coast, he had picked up some of the Punic tongue, but only enough to deal with simple matters like meat, drink and sleep. He looked at the dark waters of the inner harbour: a littered expanse of straw, fruit skins, rotting timbers and the swollen, drowned body of a dog which nudged gently against the hull of the galley as the tidal swell surged and sank. Above the bay, the evening sky was flecked with wisps of cloud, and between sea and sky were the walls of Carthage.

As Kayin climbed after the others onto the quay, staggering as the solid ground rocked beneath his feet after weeks at sea, he noticed a figure up on the city walls, apparently watching the bustle of the harbour. Moving closer, he realised that it was a girl, quite young, wearing a long white robe embroidered with silver thread which glinted in the light of the setting sun. He could not see her face clearly but he felt her eyes upon him. For a strange instant it was as if she was gazing through his clothing, through his skin and bones and into his very marrow. Shaken, he lowered his eyes, and when he ventured to glance up again she had vanished.

Someone grabbed him roughly by the tunic and the pilot of the merchant galley ordered him to help unload the cargo in part-payment for his passage. It was almost dark when he finished shifting the wine amphorae and the nuggets of gold wrapped in linen cloth, and the pilot allowed him to bed down on the deck for one more night. A sliver of moon hung over the city, reminding Kayin of the mysterious watcher on the walls and he shivered at the memory of her penetrating gaze.

Waking at cockcrow, he found Carthage already stirring. The stifling heat of midday had not yet descended and a brief, dewy freshness graced the streets and intersecting alleyways. With a few stumbling phrases, he obtained directions to the potters' workshops where he was going to offer his labour. Although they lay near the harbour, the way led through a maze of passageways; some no more than a dusty gap between two blank walls, others wide and spacious and lined with houses as many as six storeys high. Amid the hotchpotch of buildings stood temple porticoes, pillared entranceways guarding shadowy interiors, and in the distance Kayin saw the fortified acropolis of Byrsa dominating the surrounding cupolas and towers.

Crowds of men and women were already jostling each other in the main streets and Kayin marvelled at the sight of so many people—pale Celts, dark nomads from the desert regions and tall Egyptians as well as the throngs of Carthaginians. At every corner a beggar crouched—sometimes blind, sometimes missing a leg or an arm—rocking from side to side and calling out for charity. Thick clouds of flies buzzed over every rubbish heap and dung-pile, and Kayin felt his throat tighten with nausea at the filth. He had grown accustomed to the clean emptiness of the wilderness where no other men walked.

The potters' quarter, when he found it, was an untidy assortment of dwellings, storerooms and workshops stacked with slabs of bright red clay. He passed stuffy sheds where three or four men worked together, sweating in the heat as they produced rows of identical jars. Others were making oil lamps or crude statuettes of gods and goddesses, all to fill the tombs of the dead who needed tokens of household goods for their lives in the next world. Kayin was looking for the workshops of one Asdrubal, described to him as a master-potter, and eventually he found the place after many wrong turnings and blind alleys.

The potter was in the kiln room, overseeing the lighting of the huge furnace. After listening silently to Kayin's request for work in exchange for food and lodging, he answered tersely that the work was hard and the food plain, but Kayin might stay if his skills proved sufficient.

'You're no beauty,' he said, scrutinising Kayin's marred face, 'but I need another helper. You can take your bed in the workshop along with the others.'

Kayin bowed his thanks. The pilot of the merchant ship had told him that Asdrubal was one of the most highly-regarded potters in Carthage and also warned him that he was a grim-humoured man who did not tolerate fools or idlers. One of the potter's sons was ordered to show the newcomer round the place and set him to work. Smiling a warmer welcome than his father had, the young man said his name was Amilcar.

'There is my older brother, also called Asdrubal, and my younger brother Muttumbaal.' He pointed out the two at work on a large urn, the curly-haired boy turning the stone wheel in its groove while his brother skilfully moulded the wet clay. Beyond that room was a corridor stacked with shelves of unfired vases, separated by bone discs so that they did not stick together. Besides funerary urns and vases, Asdrubal's family made large terracotta statues and ornamented masks for the temple sanctuaries. Kayin turned one over in his hands, admiring the graceful lines of the girl's face detailed in the clay.

'What are these for?' he asked, choosing his words painstakingly. 'For a wife, if she is ugly, you give her a new face?'

Amilcar laughed. 'Good, very good! You're learning our language fast!' He sobered. 'The priests use them for religious rites, temple ceremonies. Look.' Replacing the girl-face on the shelf, he gave Kayin another, heavier mask with a leering mouth. The two eyes were set in a squint and on the forehead was an inverted crescent set over a disc.

'What is that?' Kayin traced the symbol with a finger.

'That? Why, that is the sign of Tanit, Lady Goddess of Carthage. What forsaken place have you been in that you haven't seen it before?'

Kayin waved the question aside. 'My story comes later. Where do I begin work?'

For the next three weeks all he saw of the city was the inside of Asdrubal's workshop and the occasional glimpse of towers and domes when he crossed the small courtyard to fetch water from the cistern. The master-potter and his sons worked arduous hours and they expected Kayin to do the same. At last a morning came when Kayin and Amilcar were dispatched to the harbour to consult with a Greek trader about a possible shipment of terracotta figurines. As they hurried through the busy streets, Kayin stopped so abruptly that his companion tripped over his heels.

'See there! Who is she?' He felt certain that the slender young woman standing on the corner was the watcher on the walls who had so discomforted him on his first evening in Carthage.

Amilcar shaded his eyes against the glare of sunlight on whitewashed walls. 'She? She's a priestess of Tanit, daughter of one of our noblest families. A great beauty.'

A priestess. Kayin stared at her as they drew closer. She was quite small—at least a head shorter than the two slave-women with her—and her black hair hung in curls below her shoulders. What drew Kayin's attention most of all was the rapt expression on her face, as if she were suspended in a state of dreaming ecstasy as she hesitated outside a booth selling incense and rare spices. Then as Kayin passed, she turned her head and once again he felt her stare. His face burned and he half-lifted a hand to hide his scar, but her luminous eyes remained fixed on him unblinkingly.

There is something; said Kayin to himself, *some authority, some power, something that she has.* Amilcar appeared not to notice the girl further and beckoned Kayin to keep up as they went on towards the merchant harbour.

Four days later, Asdrubal called Kayin from his work again. This time he was to accompany a slave delivering one of the highly-wrought funerary urns.

'You must make apologies because it's late,' he said, glaring at Kayin from under his heavy brows. 'I cannot afford to lose their custom. A curse on those sons of mine for their laziness!'

'But where is it going? To whom should I speak?' Kayin asked, weary of the master-potter's perpetual bad temper and impatience.

Asdrubal threw up his hands in fury. 'To the sanctuary of Tanit, of course! Speak to one of her pack of priestesses! For all your grey hairs, you're as stupid as a girl. I'd dismiss you tomorrow if I did not need the extra assistance.'

Kayin waited until Asdrubal had gone out into the courtyard and then spat on his footprints in the red dust. He further vented his anger by kicking the slave-boy waiting at the street door with the heavy urn. Whimpering, the boy lifted his burden and Kayin went out after him into the crowds. The sanctuary adjoined the city walls where they overlooked the inner harbour, and Kayin was able to find his way easily enough, although he sometimes lost sight of the boy. Passing beneath the ornamented stucco porch, they entered the temple precinct where Kayin sank gratefully into the shade of a cypress tree. He told the boy to leave the urn and find somebody to take Asdrubal's message.

'One of the priestesses, any young girl,' he added, pushing the boy towards a dark doorway across the precinct. Resting on his heels beneath a roof of cool green branches, he allowed a picture to form in his mind of the girl he had seen in the street, walking towards him with hands extended in welcome. *You are a grey-headed fool,* he told himself as he stood up to meet the slave-boy who was returning with a shaven-headed acolyte.

The acolyte regarded Kayin with a condescending smile. 'You bring your master's apologies?'

'He regrets the delivery is late,' Kayin replied stiffly.

'We hope for more than regrets next time. There are many other potters in Carthage.' The acolyte yawned. 'Ask your master to send his slaves with seven more urns by sunset. We make sacrifice tomorrow and the goddess cannot be kept waiting.'

'Urns for sacrifice?' Kayin asked, puzzled.

'We need urns for the remains. Do you imagine the grieving fathers will throw the bones of their little ones in the harbour?'

'You mean you sacrifice...'

'You make these urns and yet you don't know their use?' the acolyte sneered contemptuously. 'In worshipping the goddess, we give only our most prized possessions. The people of Carthage offer their children to the flames.'

As if a shutter had lifted in his mind, Kayin saw a clear image of Kanoch, his baby son. In his horror at the acolyte's words he could hardly speak. 'In all my wanderings...in all the years, I have never...' He found he had seized the urn; that he was hurling it at the head of the acolyte who ducked so that the clay smashed on the tiled floor. 'I will have nothing to do with such foul, such horrible practices.'

'What is this disturbance?'

'Forgive me, priestess.' The acolyte covered his crimson face in shame. 'This foreign slave, he...'

Kayin was about to protest that he was not a slave when he saw who it was who strode towards them. He knew it was the priestess girl in spite of the veil over her face and hair.

Clearly she knew him too because she caught her breath. 'You! I wish to speak with you.'

Kayin could hardly help smiling at her authority. She was so young, yet so certain of commanding obedience. 'You wish to speak to me? Now?'

'Follow me.' She was beckoning him towards the entrance from which she had just emerged. Kayin looked to the acolyte who motioned frantically that he should do as the priestess demanded. The slave-boy had disappeared. With some trepidation he went after the girl out of the precinct, along a stone-flagged passage and into a secluded yard, empty save for a twittering flock of sparrows.

Her pleated robe was fastened with an ornate belt and at her throat glittered a necklace of tiny silver beads strung with a turquoise crescent, a row of round pendants inlaid with amethyst and two inverted crescents of gold. When she moved, the silver rosettes on her earlobes winked, and the bracelets on her arms chinked faintly. On her chin Kayin noticed a tattoo—a blue reversed crescent set above a circle—but the marks were faded as if they had been made many years ago.

'I knew you were coming to Carthage.' She spoke more softly than before. 'I was watching for your ship when you saw me on the city wall.'

'I—I saw you,' Kayin stammered and sensed that his confusion amused her. 'Standing on the wall. You looked at me...'

'Who are you?' she said urgently. 'There is something—something in your face that I do not understand. I must know what it is.'

To Kayin it seemed then that an old, dark knowledge was surveying him through the girl's eyes. In that same moment he forgot Asdrubal, the slave-boy, the matter of the urns, and thought only of how he could reveal that he was indeed different, set apart from other people. He also burned to reveal how much he wanted her, how he longed to kiss the soft skin on the inside of her wrists and caress the breasts which pulled tight the front of her linen robe.

'I have been to the ends of the earth.' The words burst out of him. 'I was powerful once, a ruler of men. I built a city. I have seen...'

'And now you run errands for a potter.' The corners of her mouth tilted in the beginnings of a smile.

'I was weary, heart-sick,' Kayin went on blunderingly. 'I walked alone until I longed for the sight and sound of human life. There was a colony on the shore and a ship anchored in the bay and I came out of the night when they lit a fire on the beach.' He remembered the hiss and suck of invisible waves on the sand and how the circle of men sat frozen in astonishment as he walked towards them. 'They boasted of how far they had sailed and were angry when I laughed, but they said they would give me passage to their city. I was a potter once before in a lost, far-off time.' A fleeting image crossed his mind: an image of wind tugging a woman's hair long ago, but he could not even recall her name or when he had known her. 'I come from nowhere. I am accursed.'

The priestess' gaze was filled with pity. 'I know. I have always known.' She reached out to stroke his scarred cheek and he did not draw back. 'I have been waiting to give you the healing you seek.'

17

Elissa

Kayin stayed talking with the priestess in the little hidden courtyard until the first stars freckled the darkening sky. She told him that she was called Elissa, named for the Queen of the Carthaginians who gave her life for her people. Indeed they were standing not far from the spot where the Queen had set the torch to her own funeral pyre, now commemorated by a shrine and daily libations of wine and olive oil.

'I have belonged to the goddess, to Tanit, since I was born.' Elissa touched the tattoo on her chin. 'See, I have her mark here. I have served in the sanctuary since my twelfth year. For many years I have waited for you.'

'How can you know who I am?' Kayin said hoarsely. 'I was cut off from all other people, my life set apart...'

A look of satisfaction, almost smugness, crossed her face. 'I saw you in dreams, many times, journeying alone. Even in my dreams I could sense the blight upon you. I know how the green earth died at your touch.'

'How could you...' Kayin began, but she went on.

'When I sat in my chamber meditating on the Goddess, the visions and the knowledge of you came into my heart.' Her gaze enveloped him. 'I knew you from a distance when the ship brought you into harbour and I called to you in my thoughts and you heard me!'

She is so young, Kayin said to himself, *yet she speaks so surely of deep mysteries. And what is it—this cold, ancient presence that I feel—surveying me through her eyes with as slight a regard as if I were a stray insect?*

'It is Tanit whom I serve,' Elissa was saying, 'consort of Baal Hammon. It is her fertile womb which sustains the earth and the sea. She...' She stopped abruptly as the shaven-headed acolyte appeared in the courtyard.

'Mistress!' He was shrill with displeasure. 'Mistress, this slave should have returned to his master with the message I gave him. He should be whipped for his disobedience!'

'Message? Oh,' Elissa's tone grew weary, 'the urns. I had forgotten why he came. He is not a slave.'

'We make sacrifice tomorrow,' the acolyte complained. 'Mistress, you told me we needed urns.'

'I did, of course.' She turned hurriedly to Kayin. 'I do not know your name.'

When Kayin told her, the acolyte smirked. 'What kind of a name is that?'

'Get out of here!' Elissa flamed with temper and she pushed the acolyte away from her. 'You have interrupted my private conversation and insulted my guest...'

'Please, I should leave now,' Kayin said quickly, aware that the acolyte was staring at him open-mouthed. He hated drawing attention to himself—even the attention of Elissa the priestess—and he wanted to withdraw to a solitary place where he could ponder what she had said. He wondered whether he could possibly trust her.

Through his thoughts he heard her speaking to him. 'You must come back early tomorrow morning as Mago—'

she indicated the acolyte—'requested. You must come early.'

Then Kayin realised that he had momentarily forgotten the horrible matter of the sacrifices.

'Priestess.' In his fervour he moved to seize her hand. 'Tell me, is it true that your people, the Carthaginians, sacrifice their own children?'

She hesitated, biting the tip of her forefinger. 'You will not understand yet. Come back early tomorrow and I will meet you if I can, and we will talk further.' Reluctantly, Kayin said farewell and followed Mago back to the main courtyard. His stomach turned at the pictures his mind conjured of sacrifice—blood, small bodies withering in fire—but again and again he returned to the image of Elissa, her young, upright body standing close to him, her red lips speaking—what? Truth or lies?

He tried to enter the potter's workshop noiselessly while the others were at their supper of fish stew and cabbage, but Asdrubal was waiting for him. As Kayin stepped over the threshold, his master loosed a volley of curses and oaths.

'Filth! Son of a she-dog! The boy came back hours ago with some tale about you running off with a priestess. You have been chasing whores at my expense! My household has a good name and I will not have a foul-faced foreigner spoil it.'

Kayin's own temper boiled and he decided not to restrain himself any longer.

'And you,' he ground out, clenching his fists, 'you, Asdrubal, are a worthless, cack-handed potter. You make clumsy imitations of the work of your betters and you treat me, a true craftsman, worse than vermin. If you knew where I come from and who I really am, you would not dare speak to me as you do. I will not wait for you to dismiss me. I take myself from your service!' And he marched out, leaving the potter speechless in the middle of the dirty room.

Pacing the night streets, Kayin felt hunger gnaw at him and wondered why he had allowed his own outburst. A cold rain started falling from the clouds overhead and his bones ached. *I am not as young as I used to be,* he said to himself and smiled wryly. He could leave, travel on as he always did, finding other cities and other peoples to give him provision for a while, but even as he considered the idea, he knew he could not leave. Not until he had spoken with the girl priestess just one more time. But if he saw her again, then perhaps he would always be tormented by the memory of her face, her supple hips, her fine-boned fingers, tantalising and unattainable. *Maybe she is a sorceress and I am caught in her net of spells,* he thought, and the thought somehow pleased him.

He walked the ways of the city until first light and then hurried back to the sanctuary, confident that the priestess would receive him and perhaps offer him food and shelter. When she did come out to him, summoned by the sleepy, puzzled porch-keeper of the temple, she was angry, barely listening to his story of quarrel and dismissal.

'So you come without the urns? What excuse do you have, then, for dragging me from my bed?' Startled at her words, Kayin shook his head, having no answer he dared speak aloud.

Elissa sighed impatiently. 'We cannot speak here. This way, slave, to the incense-store.' She spoke loudly, seeing the porch-keeper still watching them, and Kayin obediently followed her into the maze of passageways and buildings. He noticed that she held her head very high as she walked.

Unlocking a small door, she led him into a cramped storeroom. It was stacked and stifling with jars and bowls of spikenard, sandalwood, cloves, thyme, myrrh and other aromatic resins and ointments that Kayin did not know.

'You must understand,' she said, as soon as she had closed the door, 'that I am a priestess under a rule of celibacy which I must not compromise. It must all happen as the goddess ordains and not otherwise.' Kayin hardly heard her.

'You are more beautiful than I remembered.' His mouth formed the words as they entered his head and he reached out to touch her arm.

She took no notice. 'You must go to your master, the potter, and ask him to take you back into his household. It is not yet time for you to leave.'

Tormented by the longing inside him and baffled by her behaviour, Kayin groaned, pressing his palms against his aching forehead. 'Explain yourself, Priestess. I have not slept and I am very tired. I came back as you asked and you are angry with me. Explain your hints and secrets or I will leave.'

Gently, she took hold of his fingers and placed them between her cool hands. 'Forgive me. I have thought about you and waited for so long that I forget that you know nothing. Sit beside me.' She patted one of the bulging sacks spilling scented white dust onto the floor. 'The people here think they know Tanit, Lady of Carthage. She has priests and priestesses to serve her and rituals performed in front of all the city, but most do not really believe. Instead of worshipping, they think only about satisfying their own greed, wanting more wealth, more power for themselves.'

'And the sacrifices—the children? You let them die for other men's greed?' Kayin could not hide his disgust.

Running a hand through her hair distractedly, Elissa stood up. 'That is all part of the same corruption—not as it should be. You must understand that there are deeper mysteries. The goddess gives life, not death. She is mother of us all, but I alone seek the full truth of her.' She told again of how she brooded on the goddess as she wandered the temple courts and how she was granted a vision of Kayin. 'I saw you, then, and my heart said that you were to be my consort. Through you and me the glory and fruitfulness of the goddess will be loosed on the earth. As the priests say, Tanit releases the power of Baal Hammon.'

Kayin felt a pulse beating at his throat. 'How is this to be?'

'It will be easy. You will lie with me and I will conceive a child. When they discover I have broken the rule of celibacy, they will throw me out as a whore.'

'They?'

'The priests, and my father. You will come forward, willing to take the defiled priestess as your wife, and they will release me so that we can flee the city and its politics and trade and trafficking. You will take me far away to an empty place where we will meet the goddess face to face in true worship. I have seen it all. We will return one day, when we are grown great and filled with the goddess' power.'

Watching the dust motes dance in the stripes of sunlight, Kayin whispered, 'You do not know what I have done, what lies behind me countless years ago.'

'But I know it already. You came under a curse from a cruel god, forcing you into exile and loneliness. Yet all the time your footsteps were leading you here, as the goddess ordained.' As Elissa spoke, her voice quivered with excitement.

Kayin could not answer aloud, but his heart cried silently, *Yes, that is true. I have been wronged. There is no more to tell. Not now.*

'Do you trust me?' Elissa bent forward until their eyes were level. Weak with desire, Kayin mumbled assent.

'Come back in seven nights' time,' she continued. 'I will show you a wicket gate in the wall by the harbour. Knock three times and I will open it to you. Remember, in seven nights. Not before.'

She let him out of the sanctuary through the wicket gate and he trudged back to the house of Asdrubal. The master-potter was working on the wheel and showed only by a tilt of his brows that he was surprised to see Kayin again. He listened to his faltering, craven apology and then simply nodded at him to resume work. They exchanged no further words. Joining Muttumbaal in the kiln-room, Kayin helped him unload a batch of newly-fired terracotta ware. After almost an hour of labour, the younger man broke the silence.

'I hear that when the priestesses of Tanit forget their vows, they are insatiable,' he said with an insinuating smile.

Kayin's fist struck the lad hard on the mouth so that he crashed backwards into a stack of pots.

Leaning over him until their faces were almost touching, he hissed, 'If you say such things again, or if you tell your father or brothers that I hit you, I will kill you.' But as he spoke, his vision blurred and he thought for an instant that it was his own brother, Hevel, cowering before him with blood trickling from his mouth and his eyes blank with fear. Stunned, he let Muttumbaal climb shakily to his feet. Then Kayin fled to the furthest and most secluded of the storerooms where he hid in a corner, sheltered by the darkness, until the tension in his body ebbed away.

After an unimaginably slow week of monotonous days and restless nights, the time came for him to return to the sanctuary. Gradually the hours of the last evening passed as he made himself eat supper and lie down to rest in his usual place, across the workshop from the street door. At a pitch of feverish impatience, he listened as the others settled themselves, fidgeting and yawning and occasionally muttering to one another. Finally there was quiet and their breathing became regular and deeper, the calm sigh of sleep. Kayin waited until sure that he was safe and then crept off his mat and threaded his way over the bodies to the door. The creaking hinges shattered the stillness and he thought Amilcar's lids flickered, but nobody moved or spoke and Kayin relaxed.

Stepping out into the street, he saw a huge full moon hanging yellow and pendulous above the rooftops. From a nearby stable-yard he could hear the camels rumbling and belching, and further away a dog barked, as if in answer, staccato notes in the hush of the night world. He hurried down towards the harbour where the sanctuary stood, and to the wicket gate. The moonlight transformed the familiar turnings and alleyways into bewildering shadows and black shapes, and Kayin had to slow his pace to avoid stumbling and falling. Whenever other passers-by approached, he hid in an angle of shadow until they had gone.

Soon he could hear the waves slapping against the moored trading ships in the harbour and the sanctuary wall blocked his path. Brushing the wall with his fingers, he walked on until he felt wood instead of stone. Holding his breath, he knocked three times. The gate opened immediately and noiselessly, and a smooth hand seized his, pulling him inside.

'Priestess? Elissa?' he whispered uncertainly and the hand moved to cover his lips, warning him to keep quiet. Lit only by the moon, he followed the muffled figure along the edge of a courtyard and through a low entrance into complete blackness. His footfall echoed a little on the unseen floor, as if he were in some kind of hall, and he felt his guide's hand touch his elbow warningly; a touch that burned his skin like fire. There was a rustle of cloth and a tiny light appeared in the dark revealing Elissa's face illuminated from below. She had removed her veil and Kayin saw that her eyes were rimmed with kohl and her mouth rouged, exaggerating her features so that she looked more like one of the beautiful sanctuary masks than a living human being.

Beckoning to him, she held the lamp to show him the steps they had to descend, polished black marble like slabs of moonless night. The bobbing light led him down and round a corner and into a narrow, low-ceilinged room, scarcely more than an alcove. Accustomed to the dimness by now, he could see Elissa standing before him, the lamp at her feet. The air was warm and stuffy with stale incense and the faintest aroma of cooked meat.

'It is here that we can meet,' Elissa murmured. 'We meet with one another and with the goddess. Not in public display, when her altar is heaped with offerings, but here in the darkness. Come to me.'

Undoing the belt at her waist, she pulled off her robe in a single movement. She was far more beautiful than he had dreamed. Hastily, clumsily, he removed his own clothes and stepped towards her. As their bodies touched in a first, long embrace, he unfastened the ivory comb holding her hair in place and the black curls tumbled down like a skein of silk.

They lay together on their heaped garments and he covered her with kisses. Closing his eyes, it seemed to him that the garments beneath them turned to lotus flowers and scented lilies, budding and blossoming so that the alcove was filled with petals, falling like sweet rain. The girl's mouth against his tasted of ripe pomegranates and her limbs were plastered with clinging petals, and his arms embraced blossom and she was flowers, all flowers, yielding and so soft. He thought he could hear the sea again, warm waves lapping gently around them under the full moon, and he looked up and saw Elissa outstretched against a star-crowded sky. Her body spanned the heavens and her gaze turned on him like twin suns, but the light was moonlight-cold. White, cold fire. He was a god, a king, and as his body moved over hers, he felt the weight of a horned crown pressing on his brow. The white light of her gaze grew until it blazed all around him and he cried out in fear and ecstasy.

18

The Priestess and the Potter

The shell lamp burned with a steady globe of yellow light, painting the walls of the alcove with vague shadows. Kayin lay on his right side, resting on his elbow and watching Elissa who slept beside him. He studied the gleam of sweat where the lamplight fell on her skin, the pure curves of her breasts, her mouth pouting a little in repose. Leaning towards her, he ran his hand down the length of her body and she stirred momentarily, sighing, and settled into deeper sleep.

Kayin lay back, pondering what had happened between them that night. Would she tell him that he had felt the touch of the goddess? He thought of other women he had known in other times, so many whose names he had long ago forgotten—an Egyptian princess, a Persian slave-girl, the wife of an Arcadian farmer. Then his mind turned as it always did to the other: the one whom he had—loved? Yes, loved, although he had never touched her. She was the one who had offered him companionship for a time, even though she belonged to another man. Suddenly he remembered and spoke her name aloud.

'Ani.' The name brought a brief recollection of her face, but it did not move him any more. Whatever other encounters he had had, however passionate, seemed commonplace, animal coupling compared to what he had just experienced.

Looking down at Elissa, he began talking to himself half under his breath. 'Elissa. She has touched my soul, the heart of me. Elissa. I know nothing of her except that she is a priestess from a noble family. She saw me in a dream before I ever came to Carthage.' What did she see when she looked at him? Sparse, greying hair, face twisted on one side by scars, shoulders stooping with tiredness as the slow years gradually wore his strength away. Another forgotten memory surfaced in his mind. A memory of words said by an old woman in a dirty hut: 'You will wander and not find rest...it is a cloud that swallows the path ahead of you...I cannot see more.' Maybe he would pierce the cloud at last and find rest, lying at Elissa's side and wrapped in her embrace.

Suddenly her eyes were open and alert, staring up at him. Kayin smiled at her, but she did not respond with any warmth.

'We must go now, quickly.' She was on her feet before she had finished speaking, flinging on her garments, her face averted from him. Still absorbed in the mystery of the past hours, Kayin was bewildered by the abrupt change in her.

'Elissa,' he said, the word like honey on his tongue. 'Elissa, did I give you pleasure?'

It was as if she had pulled shyness and secrecy about her like a veil. 'You must hurry. Nobody must see you leave.'

'Have you nothing else to say? When shall I return?'

She looked at him without expression. 'You must not

come back without my leave. Anyone found guilty of defiling a priestess of Tanit would be severely punished.'

Kayin gasped. 'So you brought me here to serve your purposes, knowing all the while that I risk...'

'No! It is not my purpose. It is what the goddess ordains.'

'And when I claim you—when you are thrown out of the sanctuary—will not the priests say that it was I who defiled you?'

'No.' Her words were shaky with unshed tears. 'It will be...it will be in Tanit's hands. She will not fail us now that we have joined with her.'

'So you did feel...you were not...' Kayin tried again to speak his overwhelming feelings. 'There was power over us tonight. I was...changed.'

Elissa nodded solemnly. 'For me it was the same. The goddess touched us. We are both made her children.' Their hands touched and clung together, but then Elissa gently pulled away. 'Come, we must leave.'

A week later, she sent for him again, and again three days after that, and he soon learned to find his own way to the alcove, stealing through the warm night to where she waited for him. By their fourth meeting, she no longer withdrew into silence and diffidence when their love-making had finished, and Kayin saw that she was beginning to trust him. He was not merely the one chosen by Tanit and sent to the priestess to work the divine plan, but a man who touched her tenderly, cradling her face in his hands, kissing her chin, her eyelids, her forehead, the tip of her nose, telling her that she was beautiful.

Afterwards, they would lie side by side in the glow of the shell lamp and talk quietly, their hearts beating together, their arms and legs entwined. Kayin craved to know more of Elissa herself—the woman beneath the mask of dignified priestess. He urged her to tell about her past: her childhood on her father's prosperous country estate, and her girlhood in the courts of Tanit's temple. Hour by hour, she described the olive groves where she and her sisters had hidden among the ancient, gnarled trees; the orchards where bees had droned and danced among the flowers and where, later in the season, she used to steal the ripening fruit. In their thoughts, she led him along the rows of vines and through the cattle pastures, and by the edge of the irrigation streams where she liked to bathe her dusty feet.

Sometimes she would interrupt her talk, thinking she had heard a footstep in the great hall, and then Kayin would again question her confidence in her plan of escape.

'Are you certain that we could leave the city freely? That you would be thrown out of the sanctuary without any further punishment? What if the priests only give you a beating and do not let you go?'

She would shake him in mock-exasperation, her black curls brushing his face. 'You must not doubt the goddess' power! We have pledged ourselves to her and she is far stronger than the scheming men who pretend to worship here.'

Kayin would tug her hair teasingly. 'And you, Elissa? Do you care for me or do you just use me for your satisfaction? Did you spin me a tale to bring me here and make me a slave to your desires?' Elissa would crush him against her breasts, smothering his words, and they would roll over together, struggling and trying not to laugh too loudly.

Sometimes Kayin would think of the outrages committed in the name of the goddess in the very temple where they lay. His mood would turn grim, troubling Elissa who feared that he might condemn her for the part she played.

'In the old days, many more children were given to Tanit and Baal,' she would plead. 'But in those days, even the priests and magistrates believed they needed to give tribute to preserve Carthage. It is only in recent times that they have turned corrupt.'

The dream-like nights in the temple alcove interspersed days of laborious work in Asdrubal's pottery. As Kayin's fingers recovered their old skill, his contemptuous, impatient master regarded him with surprised interest which soon turned to something like awe. His sons openly praised Kayin's work, although Muttumbaal remained aloof, shuffling nervously whenever he and Kayin were alone in the same room. One day Asdrubal spent nearly three hours watching Kayin mould the features of a clay mask which was meant to recreate the harmonies of Elissa's face without betraying her identity. When the master-potter finally spoke, he used a tone of grudging admiration which Kayin had not heard before.

'You're a good craftsman. One of the best. I've seen nothing like your workmanship anywhere else. You don't follow the customary patterns and shapes.' Shaking his head, he stumped off to bully the slaves unloading the kiln.

As the months passed and the glaring heat of summer came to swallow up the city again, making the streets stink like sewers, Kayin found he had won a name for himself among the other potters of Carthage. Although some looked askance at his work, muttering that nobody would want such strange jars and pots, others praised Kayin unreservedly and a crowd would gather at the workshop door to watch him at the wheel.

Although the master-potter grumbled at them, complaining that they should get back to their own tasks, Kayin knew that he was secretly delighted with the attention. He overheard him boasting to his sons that the newcomer had made their fortunes. Women came to the workshop from all over the city to buy Kayin's shapely oil flasks and perfume phials, and they spoke disparagingly of the heavy two-handled jars brought from Tyre by some traders and offered for sale at the harbour.

One forenoon, when the sun glittered in a sky like burnished copper, Kayin heard a buzz of voices at the street door and Amilcar darted through, calling him to prepare for a meeting with a distinguished visitor.

'He's asking for the new potter. He says he has a commission for you!' Amilcar pointed excitedly towards the knot of people in the passageway.

'Who is this man?' Kayin asked, wiping his hands on a damp rag.

'Himilco, one of the wealthiest magistrates in the Court of Four Hundred. They say he'll be made a suffete one day.'

Kayin stood still, remembering Elissa telling him about her rich father who spent his life pursuing power, executive power, as one of the two suffetes or judges who ruled Carthage. She described him without love as a harsh man who imposed the city's laws without showing mercy on human weakness. His name eluded Kayin, but maybe it was Himilco.

When he saw the tall man awaiting him, he immediately recognised Elissa's wide forehead and upturned nose in his features, and knew that this was surely her father.

He also saw shrewdly appraising eyes and a cruel mouth, and was troubled by what he saw. Himilco did not look like a man who would lightly shrug off the matter of a disgraced daughter.

Hiding his uneasiness, Kayin welcomed the magistrate to the house of Asdrubal and studied the man as he replied in kind. He was dressed in the usual woollen robe and conical felt hat, made from the finest cloths and without any stain or tear. The spiral bracelets on his wrists and the ring he wore in his nose were pure gold.

'I want you to make an image for me,' he began in the tones of a man accustomed to giving commands, 'for my private chapel. A statue of Tanit, Mother-Goddess of Carthage,' he added, condescending to Kayin's possible ignorance as a foreigner.

'Which tradition would you like me to follow?' Kayin asked.

'I do not want a mere copy,' the magistrate said disdainfully. 'I have heard that you create new images and shapes. Make me an image of Tanit unlike any other you have seen. And go to the sanctuary by the harbour. One of my daughters, Elissa, is a priestess there and she will show you other images. Mine must be different.'

Caught unawares by the mention of Elissa, Kayin stammered something incomprehensible, flushing like a love-struck boy and sure that Himilco must be able to read his guilt plainly. The magistrate, however, took no notice. He gathered his three companions about him like a guard of honour and left Asdrubal's house in stately procession.

The master-potter clapped Kayin on the back, bursting with pride. 'If word gets about that Himilco wants your skill, then every magistrate and scribe in Carthage will come here, afraid of being outdone!' He rubbed his hands. 'Well, go quickly. Go to the sanctuary. You must start work as soon as you can.'

Dazed, Kayin set off along the familiar route, remembering at the last minute not to turn along the harbour wall, instead entering the sanctuary at the main gate. He was met by Mago the acolyte who saluted him respectfully this time and ran to fetch Elissa. When Kayin told her his errand, her astonishment was even plainer than it had been at his sudden appearance, unsummoned, in broadest daylight.

'Come,' she said when he had finished. 'I will show you what you ask. And,' she went on in a lower voice, 'I have something to tell you.' She led him to stand in front of the closed doors of the great hall. After making sure that no one else was around, she pulled him closer so that she could whisper in his ear. 'It is safer here. Nobody can spy on us.'

'Elissa, when I realised it was your father...'

'Shh! You must not call me by name now. Remember, I am the priestess. You must be very careful. Do not speak about my father. It is the ones like him who dishonour the goddess; men who worship money above everything else.'

'So what should I do?'

'Do what he asks, of course. He is a powerful man and when he decides something, he uses all his will to make it happen. Do not think of disobeying him without good reason!'

Kayin bent down and kissed her suddenly, savouring the touch of her cheek, as round as a ripe peach.

'Not here!' she said fiercely. 'You must listen to my news and go.'

'You have not shown me the images.'

'They are always the same; always monstrous, giant women with angry faces and swollen breasts. They are the wives whom the little image-makers long for in their secret dreams. You must make something that shows the true power of the goddess—something of what you have seen in our nights together.'

Kayin smiled. 'Surely that would be too alarming for your father.'

'Maybe.' She seemed too distracted to smile in return, visibly brimming with some kind of deeper delight. 'Kayin, I think I have conceived a child.'

'My love.' Kayin moved to embrace her just as she sprang back, looking past him down the corridor.

'Priestess!' One of the temple servers was approaching, intent on some trivial business.

'You must go,' Elissa said hurriedly, brushing aside his questions. 'We will meet again soon. The goddess watch over you.'

Moving like a sleepwalker, Kayin made his way to the pottery, his ears ringing with the news. He hardly dared hope that what she said was true; that he might see his child, his own living child. He recalled with poignant clarity the last memory he still had of Kanoch. A memory of small chubby arms locked around his neck and a little head resting in the hollow of his shoulder. Maybe, maybe this new birth would bring the healing of that hurt at long last. Then, filled with a rush of lightheartedness, he almost laughed aloud as he pictured Himilco's horror were he ever to hear that he was grandsire to a potter's child.

19

Desecration

Kayin lay wide awake in the breathlessly hot night, his mind wearily circling the problem of the image. Four weeks had passed since Himilco commissioned him and Asdrubal was nearly frantic with rage because Kayin had produced nothing. Not even a rough model to work from. In the fetid air of the workshop he had swatted at the mosquitos whining around his ears, and had tried to shape something, but each attempt had ended as a crumbled ball of clay hurled angrily to the floor. Now he could not even sleep. His thoughts were crossing and tangling into knots of despair.

The street door had swung partly open and a patch of moonlight glimmered on the worn threshold. On an impulse, Kayin got to his feet, pulled on the robe he had been using as a pillow and stepped out into the night. The moon was burning so brightly that he could hardly bear to look at it. It drained the stars of light and overlaid the shabbiest quarter of the city with a kind of luminous beauty. Although Elissa had not summoned him that night, he could not keep himself away from the sanctuary where she was probably sleeping out under the sky with her priestess companions. He told himself that he would simply walk by the wall along the harbour to be near her, no more. As always when they were apart, the thought of her tormented him. He pictured her smooth body uncovered for him, and craved to touch her; to breathe in the scented oil on her arms; to feel her hair spread loose over his chest as she held him.

Before he realised how far he had come, he was pacing the bounds of the sanctuary wall, drawing nearer and nearer to the wicket gate. Then his hand was on the latch, pushing it tentatively. It was unbolted. *Only to look inside,* he thought. *Only to stand on the pavement where she stands.* He knew the precincts so well that he was in no danger of discovery. It would be easy to hide or, if necessary, to argue that he was seeking inspiration for his image from the goddess herself. Feverishly, he fashioned excuses while his hand unlatched the gate and opened it wide enough for him to slip through. *Only to look,* he repeated to himself, almost maddened by the brilliant moonlight, by the heat so intense that it was like thick fog pressing around him, by the longing to crush Elissa against him, their bodies melding into one.

At the portals of the great hall, he halted and listened. Through the crack between the doors, shadows were flickering and he heard subdued voices, perhaps part of a ceremony taking place at the far end where the clawed feet of the brazen altar gripped the marble floor. Stepping closer, he set one eye to the crack, but the people were to one side, out of sight, and the hall was ill-lit. All he could see were the shadows moving against the western wall on his left; shadows cast by the sparking red and orange light of a large fire.

A jangle of music startled him as a chorus of voices struck up a hymn. Kayin caught enough of the words to know that they were singing to Tanit, Mother-Goddess, Lady of Carthage. A goddess ritual so late at night? Puzzled, he tried to remember the little that Elissa had told him of temple ceremony. Then he realised what he might be witnessing. There could only be one ritual so late, so secret. It must be the Moloch: when the people of the city brought their own children to give into Tanit's deadly arms.

Horrified curiosity kept him at the crack between the doors, remembering how he had once pressed Elissa to tell him what happened. The grotesque silhouettes leaping and interweaving on the wall would be the dancers, disguised as grinning demons. While the dance continued, a single male voice chanted on a high note, but Kayin could not decipher the words.

'The little ones do not suffer,' Elissa had said. 'The priest sends them into drugged sleep so they do not feel pain. Only the father and mother...' The flames reared up, suffusing the hall with a golden glow and a woman cried out, her voice cracking in an extremity of anguish. The musicians drowned the sound, bursting into a louder, triumphal song while the dancers whirled in a blur of supple limbs. 'The father and mother must not cry out,' Elissa had continued, 'or the value of the sacrifice will be diminished. They must give gladly.'

Kayin did not see the temple server until she was close enough to know he was a stranger. As she drew breath to give the alarm, Kayin struck her down and she collapsed in a groaning heap. Then he was running back to the harbour gate, carelessly crossing courtyards in the full moonlight and knocking over two slaves who tried to stand in his way. Out, out, past the inner harbour. Out along the shore and over the rocks below the city walls. He plunged into the cold, clean water, diving down until his ears sang. Then he surfaced, pulling back to the shore with slow strokes, his eyes stinging with salt.

Although his skin was cleansed and cooled, he still smarted inwardly, scalded by what he had seen. It was as if his own heart had been dipped in fire. A child's life cut off, small hands burning, innocent blood licked up by thirsty flames. A breeze touched his wet cheek like a gust from an oven, and the realisation struck him that he had to shape an image of this goddess; one who was thought to need nothing less than children as burned offerings. Elissa offered herself to a vision of power which she called Tanit and others worshipped the same goddess with a perverse love more horrible than hate.

Slowly he grew calmer, forcing his mind to focus on the original problem of Himilco's request. When he looked at Elissa, he no longer sensed the ancient presence watching through her eyes. But was that what she knew as Tanit? A strange force existing alongside her, inhabiting the same body? He shivered. It reminded him of the terrible patience of the stalking beast, certain of catching its prey in the end and content to wait as long as necessary. Perhaps that same presence was with them on the nights when they were together, descending on them like a brood mare on heat and infecting them with its frenzied desire. An image rose in front of him as if outlined above the black water. A hybrid creature—the powerful head and forepaws of a hunting lioness, and the body of a horse, rearing on its hindlegs. The face would be human—the face of Elissa transformed and empowered by ageless majesty.

As the vision faded, he knew his problem was solved. Wringing some of the water from his soaking clothes, he set off back to the workshop, determined to start immediately. The clay quickly took shape under his fingers and he worked with scarcely a pause for food or sleep, afraid that he would lose the flow of his work.

One day he went to Himilco's palatial home to see the plinth in the chapel where the image would stand. Kayin had not been inside the home of one of the wealthy Carthaginian elite and he found it overflowing with patterned carpets, silken cushions and tapestried hangings, cedarwood chests and brass pitchers. Whole rooms were panelled with costly aromatic cedarwood and one was lined with ivory banqueting couches, inlaid with silver and decorated with golden horses' heads for elbow rests. Kayin passed a slave carrying an enormous flask made of dark blue glass containing, he was told, Egyptian perfumed lotion for one of the master's daughters. Himilco's other children moved about the corridors or lounged on the terraces; sons and daughters mostly younger than Elissa and all with some measure of her beauty.

Kayin had not met with Elissa for a number of weeks, but from time to time she managed to send word that she was prospering. He found a black pebble outside the wicket gate with the sign of Tanit scratched on one side, and took it as a sign that all was well. After that, he went to the merchant harbour whenever he could find an excuse and always scoured the ground outside the little gate. Then a week and a half went by without any message or sign and he grew anxious, knowing that Elissa's secret could not be hidden much longer.

One morning he knew that something had happened—some significant event—as soon as he stepped outside the workshop. Men and women stood in the shade, clustered together in busy discussion. The usual street chatter and clamour was subdued, almost furtive, as if there was something threatening in the air. Kayin did not need to ask what the news was. His skin prickled with a sense of doom and a voice whispered deep inside him, 'It is now. The time has come.'

Before the others in the workshop could stop him, he slipped among the crowds who were all heading in the same direction, towards the sanctuary. Kayin started to run and arrived at the main entrance before many people had assembled there. The gates were closed.

'No use knocking. The High Priest ordered them shut this morning,' said one loiterer to him. Ignoring him, Kayin made himself turn back towards the pottery, even though his breathing came fast, and sweat beaded his forehead. There was nothing for him to do except wait, although he was quite sure that Elissa had now been discovered. What else could cause such a stir?

However much he tried to steady himself, he worried more and more that their plan had gone hopelessly wrong. Uneasiness nagged at him, as if Elissa were trying to tell him by power of thought alone that she was in grave trouble. All the rest of that day and the next, he heard nothing except the rumours flying around the city—the eldest daughter of Himilco was disgraced. She had broken the rule of celibacy. She had sold herself to foreign sailors below the sanctuary wall. Himilco was the laughing-stock of the Court of Four Hundred and he would never be suffete. He was overseeing the punishment of his daughter whom he had reared to be High Priestess...

As the rumours turned blacker, Kayin felt trapped in a nightmare; a horrible dream-world from which he could not wake. He had to keep his fears secret and be careful not to show more than a passing interest in events at the sanctuary, while his mind conjured dreadful possibilities about whether and how Elissa would be punished.

On the third day, when the searing afternoon was waning into dusty twilight, Amilcar came hurrying to drag him from his work. The raw clay image now rose taller than Kayin and he was trying to focus his attention on moulding the muscular rearing legs.

'Come, you must come and see this.' Amilcar swept in breathlessly. 'They're going to cast the priestess out of the sanctuary and offer her to the crowd. Everybody's going to watch. Even my father.'

Steadying his hands as he set down his tools, Kayin turned what he hoped was an impassive face to Amilcar. 'Very well. Even I get tired of clay sometimes.'

Amilcar laughed, unaware of the other's strained manner, and waited impatiently until Kayin was ready. The packed streets suggested that the whole of Carthage was out and rushing to the sanctuary. Kayin and Amilcar arrived at the rear of a sizeable crowd waiting expectantly in front of the gates.

'I've heard she's been branded on her father's orders,' said a nearby man with slow relish.

His friend blew his nose with a plump thumb and forefinger. 'I'd like to get my hands on her, branded or not.' Then the crowd hushed as the gates started to swing open with painful slowness.

Even standing near the back, Kayin could see over most of the heads as Himilco appeared in the widening gap between the gates, his expression thunderous. A small group of priests and temple officials came behind and the crowd craned forward eagerly.

Commanding total silence with a glance, Himilco said loudly, 'The defiled priestess will be cast out. She has confessed the name of her collaborator…' There was a ringing in Kayin's ears and he missed the name. He saw Amilcar's surprised face and waited for the young man to turn on him, but…

'Mago!' Amilcar was saying. 'A puny little acolyte. And a girl like her who could have had anyone! He'll pay for it.'

'…and I serve Carthage, not my own interests.' Himilco's sombre tones roused Kayin from his stupor. 'I do not shrink from judging my own daughter and I here condemn her as worthless filth. Anyone can take her.' Looking back to the inner courtyard, he called, 'Bring her out!'

The crowd stood on tiptoe and this time they were rewarded by the sight of a small, shuffling figure between two temple guards, her pregnant belly visibly outlined against her robe. Kayin stared, not even quite sure that it was Elissa.

Her beauty was ravaged. They had shorn her hair as a mark of her disgrace and her naked scalp was raw and bleeding. Above her terrified eyes, boldly imprinted on her forehead, was the word WHORE in the Punic tongue. She was scanning the crowd, probably searching for Kayin, but her gaze swept over him as if the horror and torture had made her forget him altogether.

'Who will take her?' Himilco called again. 'You can see what she is by the word she bears.'

The two men standing near Kayin stirred, as if about to speak, and without another thought Kayin shouted out, 'I will take her.' Hardly conscious of Amilcar's restraining hand, he shoved his way to the front where Himilco eyed him in cold surprise.

'I think the potter does not understand,' he said. 'She is

disgraced. Will your master let you bring such a woman to his house?'

'I will not!' Asdrubal's angry tones came from the middle of the crowd, and the people laughed.

Kayin took no notice. 'I am leaving Carthage.' He spoke quietly so that only Himilco heard. 'Your image will be finished by others. I have done what I can and now it is time for me to go.' He finally dared to look at Elissa, but her head hung down and she swayed on her feet, close to collapse.

Himilco lifted his eyebrows in exaggerated surprise. 'Take her, then. But you're a fool. You could have found yourself a good wife in the city.' Lifting his voice, he called out, 'Make way for the foolish potter and the whore!' The people laughed again, uneasily this time. They knew and respected Kayin as a skilled craftsman and did not understand why he was bringing needless shame upon himself.

Kayin took Elissa's limp hand in his and led her through the crowd. They walked through streets walled with staring men and women, some clutching stones which they dropped when they saw who it was who had claimed Elissa. Kayin urged her on in a whisper to which she did not respond. She merely trudged beside him until they came to the workshop. Kayin went inside for the last time to collect his few possessions, packed ready for such a departure. From the heap of bedding in the corner, he picked up a ragged shawl to cover Elissa's poor, shamed head. Then he took her hand again and they left, taking the broad street leading through the heart of the city and onto the road for the south.

20

Daughter of the Goddess

They followed one of the trading routes which wound away from Carthage deep into the desert and on, so other travellers told them, to remote tropical lands. At first the way led them through groves of olive and almond trees, their leaves wrinkled and dusty after long months of scorching heat. Sometimes they walked along marshy valleys filled with rustling date palms and grazing herds of oxen.

At all times Elissa kept her face hidden in the shawl Kayin had given her and did not speak a single word, only nodding or shaking her head when he offered her food or rest. At night they slept under the open sky, their bodies never touching because she flinched from any contact except the joining of their hands at the start of each day's journey. Kayin continued to walk south, simply because it was the easiest way to leave the city without crossing water. He did not know whether he really believed in Elissa's goddess and her talk of power and revelation, but he knew that he loved Elissa and wanted to do everything he could to help and heal her.

And I am not alone, he said to himself. *Even though I am wandering homeless again, I have somebody with me. She will recover and then there will be the child.*

Whenever they came to one of the dome-roofed mud villages strung along the route, Kayin would leave Elissa in a patch of shade and go in search of food. When his begging met with kicks and curses, and his hoard of coins with blank stares, he would steal something, knocking a hole in a crumbling granary wall or bullying a frightened girl into giving him bread. Once he returned to find Elissa sitting with a lapful of artichokes, garlic and figs. They had been thrust into her hands by a crowd of friendly children.

On another day they came to an almost deserted village where a few old women sat by their tumbledown houses, slapping at flies. On that day, Elissa was close to collapse through tiredness and hunger, and she allowed Kayin to take her right into the village. At the first house they came to, a kindly grandmother made them eat a dish of porridge with honey and cheese, hovering around them and exclaiming anxiously as they did so.

'You must not travel far in this heat, not with a child on the way,' she said to Elissa who did not reply.

Kayin smiled apologetically. 'We are on family business.' He looked around the bare, gloomy room, furnished with a terracotta brazier for cooking and two chipped jars. The dish of porridge was probably the only food in the house.

One morning they were trudging along under the hot sun when Kayin, irritable with hunger, snapped at Elissa, 'Maybe the chosen ones—those close to the goddess like you—do not grow famished. Did you bring me here to starve me?' Startled, she raised her face to his and he saw suddenly how thin her cheeks had become.

'Tanit—she will look after us,' she said slowly.

Kayin gave a short, disbelieving laugh, but when they

had gone on for another hour or so, he heard hooves behind, approaching briskly. A boy on a donkey came into sight, loaded with woven panniers of fruit. As he was about to pass them, the boy suddenly leaned over and pulled two ripe pomegranates from the panniers and tossed them at Elissa's feet. Then, without a word, he kicked the donkey into a faster trot and disappeared in a cloud of dust.

As they went further south, fields and plantations gave way to stone and scrub and expanses of sand-coloured rock. Sometimes it was hard to find even a bush to crouch under for a little shelter at noon. Kayin wondered how much further they could go, but when he questioned Elissa, she merely shook her head.

'Not here. Still too many people. She is calling us to the heart of the desert.'

Kayin tried to answer her patiently. 'We cannot just walk on into the desert. We must have some kind of shelter and food and water; enough for both of us or we will die.'

Elissa's lips moved and he barely caught her murmur. 'She will protect us.'

The barren plains which they now crossed were rimmed by mountains and the two travellers passed hill-sides honeycombed with cell-like dwellings and fortified granaries. Sometimes they saw nomad encampments, black and brown tents and flocks searching for pasture nearby.

'This is a desolate country,' said Kayin.

'One day the goddess will make it green, all green.' Elissa almost smiled as she replied. 'When her power is freed, you will see. She gives life, not death. Remember.'

'How can you believe so certainly?'

Elissa pulled her shawl over her mouth so that her words were muffled. 'There is nothing else left.'

A few days later, they topped a hill and saw below them the clustered palm trees of an oasis. The waterskin was almost empty and Kayin was about to hurry on to find the spring, when Elissa pulled him back.

'Wait.' She pointed out to the southern horizon where the heat haze danced on the silver-grey desert. 'We must go there. She is calling us. Can you not hear?'

Kayin saw that her eyes were fixed fiercely where she pointed. 'Elissa, we cannot...'

She began stumbling down the steep hillside towards the trees, calling back over her shoulder, 'They are waiting for us by the blue water. We must hurry or they will be gone.'

As Kayin hurried after her, he suddenly checked his stride, staring in disbelief. Among the trees, sheltering under the fringed leaves from the sun, was a crowd of merchant traders and their laden horses.

Before she was noticed, Elissa drew back to Kayin's side. 'You must ask them if we can travel with them.'

The traders stopped talking when they caught sight of the travellers and crowded closer round the clear pool so that Kayin could not come near it. When he asked if he could fill his waterskin, they moved aside reluctantly.

'Where are you going?' he asked a young man wearing large gold earrings who looked less surly than the others.

'Sabratha,' he said, naming a trading-post in the far south. His companions scowled as if their destination should have stayed secret.

'We are not brigands,' said Kayin quickly. 'She—' he indicated Elissa who shrank behind him—'and I are going south too. Maybe we could share part of the road?'

'And what will you give us in exchange for our protection, our food and shelter in our tents?' said one of the older men, leering at Elissa.

To Kayin's surprise, he found himself saying in reply, 'I will tell you stories. A story each night in exchange for whatever you give us.'

'Tell us one now,' said the leering man and his friends laughed. Kayin drew breath and without any forethought embarked on the story of how he had survived the terrible Deluge so long ago. He told it from the night of the first roaring hurricane to the moment when the marsh-dwellers found him. When he had finished, the traders applauded him.

'A good tale!' The boy with the earrings grinned at Kayin. 'We have food enough for such a fine storyteller, I think.' The others agreed, nodding and smiling at Kayin, making room for him at the centre of their circle and offering him baked meat and herbs. Round the cooking fires that night, as the big stars came out one by one in the powdery darkness, he told them the story of the building of the tower and how the curse confused the people's speech. Later, he and Elissa slept in blankets by the warm embers while in the distance a pack of jackals howled at the new moon.

The merchants set off before dawn each morning so that most of their journey was done before the hottest part of the day. Leaving Carthage at summer's end, they would return in the spring with a load of furs and ostrich-skins and precious stones. They had left the city before Elissa's disgrace was made public, but Kayin still took care to conceal her identity.

She was allowed to ride one of the horses and sat motionless and uncomplaining as it jogged along over the sandy ground, following the faint trail. Although she seemed calmer than before, Kayin was disturbed at a gradual change in her eyes. They seemed to stare blankly, taking no notice of the land through which the traders were passing. Once again, as in the days when he first knew her, he felt the strange, ageless presence in her, turning her gaze to a consuming inner vision. Every trace of the proud girl he once knew had been burned away by her sufferings at the temple, the branding and the casting-out. As to what was left, he could not say.

Then, one morning, she brought the caravan to a halt after a single hour of riding. 'We must go that way.' She pointed in a south-westerly direction.

'That leads nowhere. You're mistaken.' One of the traders brought his horse alongside hers and peered doubtfully across the waste.

'Surely we must go due south with the caravan,' Kayin said pleadingly, dreading her answer.

He had to put his head close to hers to catch her whispered reply. 'She is calling us. We must go that way, you and I.'

Kayin did not spend long trying to dissuade her, telling himself that he would see the matter through to the end, whatever that might be. The traders did not hide their conviction that the storyteller's woman was crazy and they even tried to persuade Kayin to leave her behind. When he refused every offer, they embraced him and gave him blankets, water and a bundle of dried tunny fish and fresh figs. They told him that it was four days' journey on foot to the next oasis if he followed their path.

'We may meet you there,' they said, intimating that Kayin would, if he had any sense, change his mind and abandon the mad, maimed girl. Elissa tugged at his hand, urging him off into the trackless emptiness while the traders were still adjusting bridles and checking their loads. She walked heavily, often stopping to rest and leaning on Kayin's arm, although he was also carrying provisions for both of them.

The ground was bone dry and burning through the worn soles of their sandals as they crawled like ants under the vast dome of the sky. Away from the noise of hoof and harness and human chatter, Kayin became aware of the dead silence of the desert, swallowing up the small sounds of their shuffling feet and Elissa's laboured breathing. When the sun blazed at the zenith of the dome, he could bear no more and made Elissa rest beneath one of the blankets draped over two heaps of brushwood. Long before he felt ready to carry on she sat up and said they must leave.

'Little one, where are we going?' Kayin asked, his throat raw for want of a drink. He dared not even sip from a waterskin until they had some hope of finding a fresh supply.

'I know where.' The cold presence was there in Elissa's voice, compelling him to obey.

They walked on and as evening drew near, Kayin noticed a dark smudge in the diminishing heat haze ahead of them. A while later, he could see the outline of trees. An oasis. He almost wept with relief when Elissa announced that they must stop there and wait. When they finally arrived, she sank to the ground with her back against one of the tufted tree trunks and only drank a little of the water he brought her.

Am I crazed or is she? Kayin asked himself. No answer came.

Darkness fell quickly and after they had eaten a few

bites of food, he covered Elissa with both the blankets and settled himself to keep watch over her. The night quickly turned cold and he shivered, but he could not fight sleep for long and his eyelids soon drooped and closed.

He was woken by a cry. Jerking upright, he found himself in a moonless night of almost impenetrable dark. After a while, he could just make out the form of Elissa, up on her hands and knees and moaning.

'What is it?' Kayin knelt beside her, trying to gather her in his arms.

She fought him off. 'Leave me alone! You must not see!' When he tried to protest, she screamed at him, calling him evil names and wrenching herself away, staggering off into the trees until he lost sight of her in the gloom.

Waves of exhaustion swept over him and he realised that he was almost asleep on his feet. An inner voice told him that he ought to run after Elissa, to stand by her in whatever crisis had come upon her. Another, louder voice spoke of the need for sleep. Had not Elissa screamed at him to leave her alone? Resentment nagged at him. The girl must learn that although he was her lover, he was not her slave.

'Very well,' he said aloud. 'If you do not want me with you, I shall leave you alone.' Unsure whether Elissa was near enough to hear him, he repeated his words and then tried to put her from his mind as he curled up on the ground. He fell asleep almost immediately.

When he woke again, he was lying in sunshine and apart from a breeze stirring the fronds of the trees, the oasis was silent. His first thought was for Elissa and he dragged himself upright, clinging to a trunk until the dizziness of extreme hunger cleared from his head. Then, step by cautious step, he searched for her.

He found her on the far side of the pool, collapsed in a mess of her own blood and water. In her arms she held a tiny scrap of flesh—a dead child. Even Kayin could see that it had been born too early to live. She had wrapped it in a strip torn from the hem of her robe and as she sat, she was singing snatches of what sounded like a lullaby.

When Kayin choked in horror, she laid a shaking finger to her lips. 'Hush, or you will wake her.' Lifting the bundle, she held it towards him. 'A girl child, but so small, so very, very small. She is tired, she is cold, she is sleeping now until the goddess comes and breathes warmth into her. The goddess is coming. I can feel her on the wind.'

Kayin turned and walked back to where their belongings were scattered on the coarse grass. Unfastening the waterskin, he drank deeply. From across the pool he could still hear the lullaby to the dead baby. Had she lived at all, his daughter? Had she seen starlight, felt the touch of water on her skin? He would never, ever know.

Something interrupted his thoughts. The wind was bringing him a message—something he could not quite decipher. The feathery tree-tops stirred and this time Kayin recognised the smell that hung on the breeze. Smoke. Pushing his way out into the open, he scanned the flat horizons. No sign of any human encampment to the north, south or east. Then on the western rim of the sky he saw a long ragged line; black vapours rising in the morning air. The tinder-dry desert scrub was on fire.

After an instant of surging panic, he began calculating their chances coolly. If they left at once, they might outpace the fire for a while, but to where would they run? Their only hope of survival was to stay where they were and make a firebreak around the oasis. He had encountered such bush fires before in his journeyings and knew what he should do.

Back by the pool, Elissa was hunched over her pathetic little bundle. No need to disturb her yet. He set to work, tearing up bushes and branches and laying a row of kindling between the grove of trees and the path which the fire would take. Striking a spark from the flint he carried, he coaxed a small flame into life and it was soon licking its way along the piles of bark and leaf. As he ran to and fro, beating out stray cinders which threatened to ignite the nearby trees, he kept watch on the horizon where the line of smoke was thickening, veiling the sun and casting a haze over half the sky. A bush fire could outpace a running man. Before long an orange glow was visible on the underside of the smoke-pall and the wind freshened to a gale which tossed the palm-fronds like wheatstraw.

He was so busy making the firebreak that he did not notice Elissa until she was standing next to him, still holding her bundle tightly.

'We must go now.' Her face was rapt. 'She is coming. I can feel her presence about us.'

Kayin seized her arm and pulled her back into the sheltering trees. 'Elissa, it is a great fire and we must hide ourselves here in the water, otherwise we will burn.' To his surprise, she merely nodded and allowed him to lead her to the pool. Clearly she was wounded and sick in spirit and did not know what she was saying for much of the time.

Making sure they were both soaked with water, he drew her down to crouch beside him in the shallows. The fire was so close that he could hear its voice: a throbbing roar which shook him to the bone. The choking clouds of smoke seemed to pulsate around them and Kayin pulled both their heads lower to find air enough to breathe.

A moment later, Elissa tore herself from him, scrambling out of the water and through the trees. He leapt after her, but she moved faster, her wet robe flapping around her legs. She was heading straight for the oncoming flames, running like a frightened deer.

'Elissa!' he called frantically, and she glanced back, her features distorted like the demon masks of clay he had once moulded.

'She is here! I feel her touch. Come!'

'Elissa!' he called again, hopelessly. She took no notice.

'We...must...touch...her...and...live...for...ever!'

The words floated on the breath of the fire. Clearing the trees too late, Kayin saw her outlined against the scarlet and gold walls of the blaze as she rushed into the goddess' deathly embrace.

21

A Desert Place

The pilgrim lay in silence, perhaps contemplating the scene he had just described. I waited too, scarcely aware of the voices of my brothers chanting their mid-morning prayers in the oratory. I saw something glistening on the old man's cheek and heard a sigh as if he were rehearsing an old grief, almost worn out in the passage of years. Then his hand moved impatiently and rubbed away the tear and he turned back to me.

'Surely thou art tired, my son? Art thou not weary of listening to a dying man's story?'

'No, no, my Father,' I tried to reassure him. 'We often keep night vigils here, and fast too. You must finish your tale. Tell me, how did Kayin escape?'

'As thou wouldst escape such a fire. He threw himself into the pool and held himself under as long as he could bear. When he surfaced, the fire had gone, licking hungrily over the scrubland and leaving desolation behind.'

The trees of the oasis were scorched, hanging down limply like the fingers on a dead hand. Of Elissa he found no trace, although he clawed at every heap of ashes with his bare hands until they were blistered. Elissa had vanished.

Again and again he recalled the moment when the fire swallowed her. Had he seen her fall? Had she somehow leaped through the flames and was searching for him somewhere, crazed with fear? He called her name to every horizon, but in the emptiness after the fire, his voice was no louder than a bat's squeak.

Eventually he crumpled onto the ground a little way from the oasis. The thought came to him that perhaps the goddess had indeed come, as Elissa foretold, and had taken only the priestess and left behind the doubting, accursed potter.

'Take me too!' he cried to the clouded sky. 'Have mercy and take me! We two are one. Do not leave me alone!' No answer came. The clouds seethed above his head and the wind howled across the waste, blinding him with ash and sand. A spattering of rain fell, but the wind was driving the clouds north, away from the desert where there were no green plants to soften the rocks.

Then Kayin despaired and lay with his face crushed against the ash-strewn earth. He longed for death and groaned aloud as the full weight of his sorrow overwhelmed him. Elissa was gone, leaving him in a barren land, pinioned by the curse. The future yawned before him—futile years of waiting for the blight to strike again, and again, and again.

If I cannot die, he said to himself, *then I shall cut myself off from the living world. I shall hide here in the desert until my days come to an end or the world itself decays into dust.* Lifting his voice, he shouted into the silence, 'I will become nothing, just as I desire nothing.' And he closed his mouth and spoke no more.

He did not die, although he stretched himself out beneath the hot sun, renouncing all claim on his life and resolving never to eat or drink again. Somehow his body endured, hardening into a husk which held his spirit like a seed rattling in a withered pod. As the link between body and spirit weakened, his vision became keener and his senses extraordinarily clear, while above him the sun and moon brought day and night in turn. Their passage was so swift that at last he noticed them no longer and lay wide awake in a never-ending present. The light burned all around him and turned the sand and rock the colour of warm honey.

In this endless, honey-coloured present he listened to the strange music of the stars, sometimes louder, sometimes on the very edge of hearing. He watched the spirits of the earth and the heavens warring against each other and the souls of dead men and women leaving the circles of time and space. Sometimes he thought he saw human faces there in the wilderness, but as they came closer, he saw that they were really monstrous creatures—birds with feathers like burnished metal and long talons like vultures, or scarlet lions whose tails were the venomous tails of scorpions. They would pass near without harming him and then he would be alone again with the dust-devils skittering across the waste, dancing and falling in the wind.

Sometimes the wind brought him the reverberations of the human world, the tumult of nations, of empires and great cities. Out in the desert the tumult was no more than a faint murmuring, soothing him into vague dreams which began to merge with his waking moments until he wondered whether he was dead after all. Perhaps death was no more than a kind of troubled sleep.

A voice roused him. It was a distant, oddly familiar voice which beat upon his ears, speaking words he could not quite hear. It tantalised him, teasing him from the coils of sleep so that he came to a kind of consciousness of himself lying on the rock and sand beneath a sunset sky. The sun was sinking towards the western rim of the desert, painting a shimmering blood-red trail on the ground which led to the heart of the dying day. Kayin blinked and the light changed to starless night. The rocks trembled beneath him and he heard the echo of a terrible groaning in the air as if somewhere a heart was breaking.

Suddenly he heard the voice again, commanding and loud. 'Awake, sleeper, awake. Now is the day.' The newly-risen sun shone on his right hand turning the desert gold and warming the life back into him.

His voice returned to him and he spoke to the morning air. 'Now is the day.' The thought came to him that a path was set before him and that he must take it. A path into the morning. He was on his feet without realising that he had moved, and he was walking the golden path of the sun feeling new-born, every sense clean and purged and sharp. Looking down as he walked, he saw that his clothes were limp, bleached rags and his skin was seared and seamed like old leather, but at every step he took, fresh life tingled through him.

'Now is the day.' As he walked, he saw mountains rearing over the horizon and he sped along the golden path until they blotted out the sun and he halted. Surveying the peak in front of him, he saw a broad spur of rock like an outflung arm, and above the spur was a dark hole, a cave mouth. In the cave mouth was a human figure watching him.

As Kayin drew closer, he saw that it was an ageing man, face burned dark by the desert sun, white hair hanging untidily over a high forehead, skinny frame draped in a shapeless garment woven from some kind of stiff, brown fibre. When he was standing a few feet below him, the man leaned forward, surveying the newcomer and nodding his head as if satisfied. Beckoning Kayin to follow, he led him into the cave mouth which became a tunnel bringing them out into a level open space almost like a courtyard. It was partly roofed by an enormous palm tree growing in the very middle. A small stream bubbled out of a crack in the rocky floor. Kayin realised with a shock of surprise that the man was wearing cloth woven from shredded palm leaves.

Still in silence, the man motioned for Kayin to be seated and handed him a sticky mess of dates. Kayin ate them slowly, letting the sweet taste fill his mouth. He followed the man's example in drinking from the stream and washing the dust and sand from his hands and feet.

'You were waiting for me,' he said at last, searching for words after his long silence and unthinkingly using the speech of his far-off childhood days on the plateau. Somehow he was not startled when his host understood and replied in the same tongue.

'I saw you in a dream. I will not ask you for news, for I can see you have not come from the habitations of men.'

'A voice called me from the wilderness. Called me from sleep.' Kayin looked at the calm man and something of his old desperation returned. 'Do you know where I can find rest? I wanted to sleep. Sleep without waking.'

'I have lived as a hermit in the solitude of the desert for many years,' the man said. 'I have suffered and wept and cried out to heaven, and then Christ granted me His kiss of peace.'

'Christ? What is Christ?'

The hermit blinked once and said slowly, 'If we seek

God, He will appear to us. If we hold on to Him, He will stay with us. God touches man with the hands of His Son, the Christ.'

Kayin frowned. 'I have no liking for gods. Their touch brings only harm and sorrow.'

The hermit patted Kayin's head, as one would do to a child. 'Stay with me a while. I truly believe that God Himself has called you from the desert. Rest here and wait for your path to become clear. I will ask no questions and pass no judgements.'

Kayin stayed there for three days, becoming accustomed to sleeping at night on a rustling couch of palm leaves and taking a few mouthfuls of food and drink. The hermit spent his hours in silent meditation unless Kayin spoke to him. He often knelt in prayer or even prostrated himself on the ground, worshipping or interceding or making confession to his god. Once, Kayin ventured to question him.

'Are you not afraid to approach your god so openly? Do you not think He might strike you down for daring to raise your hands to Him?'

The hermit smiled. 'If your cloak were torn, would you throw it away?'

Kayin pulled a wry face because his own clothes were very ragged. 'I think I would patch it and wear it.'

'Well, if you would spare your cloak, surely God would have mercy on His own image. We are the handiwork of God. He will not cast us out.'

Turning away with misery welling in his heart, Kayin thought the hermit an old fool. He knew nothing of El, the one God who had blighted his life.

On the fourth day, he woke before sunrise. In his sleep he had heard the voice calling to him again, but this time he could not decipher the words, however hard he listened. Sitting up on his bed of palm leaves, he noticed that the hermit's resting place was already empty. He pulled on his outer tunic and walked to the stream to splash his face with the icy water. Then he stood still under the old palm tree, listening to the wind among the branches.

'Be faithful to the road at your feet.' The hermit spoke from behind him and made him jump. As the pale dawn sky arched above the courtyard, he thought of the road he had travelled already, far longer and harder than the hermit could ever guess.

'But where is it taking me now?' he asked, unable to keep an edge of mockery from his voice. 'Can your god tell you that?'

'The nearest way is the road to Alexandria,' the hermit said in a matter-of-fact way. 'From there you can take a ship to anywhere in the world. You will know where to go.'

'And you are staying here?'

The hermit chuckled. 'I would forget my own name in the busy city, in all the noise and confusion! No, I shall stay beneath my palm tree. Perhaps God will call others from the desert and I must be here to receive them.'

When the day was blue and gold with light, Kayin left the hermit, carrying some dates in a square of woven palm leaf. He walked fast and the sun had not yet grown too hot for travelling when he found he was approaching the edge of the wilderness where it overlapped with cultivated oasis groves and beaten pathways.

22

The Road to Rome

Kayin stood on the waterfront at Alexandria, bewildered by the size and splendour of everything he saw. The furled linen sails of the ships in the harbour were like a huge flock of gulls. Around him swarmed a crowd drawn from many races and nations speaking a babble of languages, not one of which he could understand. He tried to remember what Carthage had been like and tried to recall how he had once lived among men and women. But surely Carthage had never been so daunting, so large, so teeming. He was starting to piece together some of the Greek used by the people as a common tongue, and overheard talk about cities and rulers whose kingdoms stretched further than the greatest domain of ancient days. *Maybe I am growing old,* he said to himself. *It is all too much to comprehend.*

When he first arrived in Alexandria, he had managed to steal a cloak, tunic and sandals, and he had cut his hair so that he would escape notice in a crowd. With a few words of Greek, he now hoped to find himself a place on a ship, although he had no clear idea of where to go. Gathering his courage, he approached a group of sea-bronzed men chatting on the quay and asked if there was a ship's master among them.

One standing on the edge of the group nodded at him. 'Where are you bound?'

'Where are you sailing?' Kayin countered.

'Rome.'

Rome. He knew the name from his Carthage days. Clearly its influence had grown during his time in the wilderness. Now it was a seat of empire according to the gossip in the crowds. The men were waiting for a reply, wanting to get back to their own talk, and on the spur of the moment he decided to ask for passage to Rome.

'I would...sail with you,' he said haltingly.

The ship's master eyed him up and down. 'Do you have an exit pass?' He had to repeat the question three times before Kayin understood.

'I will work for passage. Help you sail,' he replied. The men muttered to one another and the ship's master scowled.

'I have a full crew here. Don't try to steal other men's work.' As Kayin began to protest he went on, 'Either you have a pass and money to pay for deck space or you have not. I don't want beggars loitering near my ship.'

Kayin stepped back, reddening with anger. 'I have no money, but I...'

'Then go! Don't waste my time!' The ship's master turned his back and started talking to his crew again, affecting to ignore Kayin who strode away, boiling with fury and longing to knock the man into the dirty waters of the dock. The sun was sinking west and the chill breeze made him shiver. With the thought of finding a warm place to shelter for the night, he started back towards the city streets, telling himself that he would return early next morning and find another ship to take him somewhere.

As the day faded, the lighthouse at the mouth of the

harbour shone out over the water, rivalling the setting sun. An old woman saw him gazing at it and nudged him with her elbow. 'That's one of the seven wonders of the world, they say.' He was about to run after her and ask for a bite of supper and a bed, hoping her friendly words signified a kind heart, but he lost her in the throng hurrying homewards.

Noticing an alleyway on his right, he pushed towards it and found it led in the same direction as the packed main street. He walked quickly past dingy walls, his sandals squelching on the slimy ground, until he heard ahead of him sounds which suggested a fight in progress. Heavy breathing, a grunt of pain, feet scuffling and stamping around the next corner. Edging forwards, he saw a young man, maybe twenty years old, struggling with two older men, one of whom clutched a knife. The young man was gasping for breath, but still managed to wriggle free of his assailants. One of the other men lunged at him again and Kayin jumped out from his hiding-place.

For a few seconds, the four of them stood frozen and then the man with the knife retreated, calling to his companion to leave the rich boy and look for easier pickings. They ran off together, knocking Kayin sideways. As they passed, he saw the knife flash and rolled away so that the blade sliced thin air. Getting to his feet, he realised the young man was watching him somewhat anxiously.

'I will do you no harm,' he said, and deliberately turned his back to brush at the filth on his cloak. The young man did not take his opportunity to leave.

'Thank you, my friend.' He spoke Greek with a trace of an unfamiliar accent. 'I was stupid enough to let those fellows lure me down here. After three years in this city I should know better.'

Kayin decided to try him for offers of help or money and explained his difficulties at the harbour, and how he wanted to take a ship for Rome.

'You have not been here long then?' the young man asked. 'You do not look like a beggar.' Then he checked himself. 'Forgive me—I always talk too freely and too fast. I am also going to Rome, so come and drink wine at my lodging-house and I'll explain how you can get passage. My name is Caius,' he added over his shoulder as he set off back towards the harbour. 'Come, it's not far to walk.'

When they emerged in the main street, a grizzled white-skinned man ran up to Caius and burst into a long, scolding speech in a language which Kayin guessed must be Latin. Caius replied in soothing tones, evidently describing his misadventure and pointing out Kayin as his saviour.

'My servant Titus,' he remarked in Greek. 'He has some unpronounceable name in the barbarous speech of his own northern country. He thought at first that you were kidnapping me.'

Titus led the way to the lodging-house which overlooked the broad sweep of the harbour and the distant lighthouse, a bright beacon in the surrounding dark. Filing into the crowded front room, they settled in a corner while Titus went to fetch wine.

'I return to Rome after studying at the Museion here,' Caius began, radiating confidence and goodwill now that the memory of the fight was fading. 'I haven't seen my wife or family for two years. When I left, my wife was fourteen years old and now she'll be a full-grown woman. And you? You have family in Rome?'

Kayin fabricated a story about travelling in the desert,

brigands, fire and loss. 'I have nothing left. Even my—my wife died. So I go to Rome for a new life.'

'Rome is not a good place to go if you haven't money or friends. And you need food, shelter and a servant if you want to cross the sea in any comfort. It's a long voyage.'

'I always find my own way,' Kayin replied stiffly. He felt old and exhausted next to Caius with his cheerful smile and energetic frame. Titus returned with the wine and after drinking in silence, Kayin stood up.

'Thank you for the wine. I take my leave.' He wanted to creep away into the shadows where he could brood on his sad, wasted life. It was cruel torture to encounter someone who looked as if he knew nothing of suffering or betrayal; whose life surely stretched before him like a long summer's day.

'But wait, my friend!' Caius was hurt at Kayin's abrupt farewell. 'This is foolishness. We are both going to Rome. You have no money and my father gives me more than I can spend, so come with me. You saved my skin this afternoon, so you can at least let me pay for your passage.'

Caius' generosity was such that when he realised Kayin had nowhere to sleep that night, he insisted that they share his bed at the inn. He spoke to Kayin as if he thought him rather simple-minded, or at least naive. He probably assumed that Kayin had never stayed in a city before. Certainly Kayin found Alexandria a daunting place. How could he begin to explain about the other cities he had seen so long ago?

In the morning, Caius escorted him to the city governor's office to get a letter of authorisation for the port officials, so that they would issue Kayin an exit pass. The young man even paid the eight drachmae fee and searched out the ship's master who had dismissed Kayin so carelessly the day before. Kayin was amused to see the man nodding deferentially and darting amazed glances at him, wondering how he had found such a liberal benefactor. Indeed, Caius was so open-handed and moved by what he imagined Kayin's plight to be, that by the end of that day Kayin was his trusted travelling companion.

'So terrible to lose your wife and your goods and almost your own life too—but maybe you would have preferred to die rather than survive such a catastrophe?' And he tried in his youthful way to make amends for what he thought had happened. He set himself to show Kayin the sights of Alexandria, second city of the Roman Empire, crossroads of the whole world. They visited the gardens, the lecture halls and even the menagerie of the Museion where students came to study literature, mathematics, astronomy and medicine. They saw the tomb of Alexander and the world-famous libraries. With Titus in anxious attendance, they climbed to the hill-top sanctuary of Pan and gazed over the whole city, while Caius explained its role as the nexus of trade for the empire, dealing in goods from lands further east than Parthia, on the very edge of the maps.

'Cottons, silks, perfumes, papyrus, spices—they all pass through Alexandria. For my wife,' and Caius smiled fondly as he mentioned her name, 'for Prisca, I have bought two ivory combs.'

After several days' wait, Kayin was woken one morning by a herald calling under the windows of the inn. Caius stirred beside him.

'He says our ship sails with the tide,' he mumbled sleepily. 'The omens are good and they have sacrificed a bull to Poseidon.'

When they got to the dockside, Kayin was astonished

at the size and beautifully curving lines of their ship, the Isis, which had a gilded goose-head on the stern and on the prow a figure of the goddess Isis. A huge crowd of maybe four hundred people crammed the quay with their piles of baggage and Titus stood among them, guarding his master's heap of bedding, clothing, and the pots and pans and provisions needed for the voyage.

Somebody tapped Kayin's arm and he saw a man at his side with a twitching, worried mouth and lined forehead.

'Excuse me,' he said, 'but can you reassure me? Was it a bull they sacrificed? I've heard Poseidon prefers bulls and I meant to make sure last night, but I forgot and then I was so afraid of dreaming about bulls that I didn't sleep at all, and now I'm in a dreadful way.'

'Bulls?' asked Kayin, who had followed the torrent of Greek with difficulty.

'Well of course you mustn't dream of bulls because that means storms, and if you dream of them goring someone, that means shipwreck.' The man sounded indignant at Kayin's ignorance. Then he gasped, staring up at the ship's rigging. 'A crow up there on the ship! Can you see it? Has the ship's master seen it? I cannot sail today. Not with a crow in the rigging. Excuse me.' Kayin squinted up at the black bird perched near the mast and shrugged, but the worried man had disappeared.

The crowd surged up the gangplank and Kayin struggled to keep close to Caius and Titus who were pressing ahead to find a sheltered patch of deck. He noticed the ship's master escorting a few elderly men on board, their wealth evident in their jewelled fingers and fine garments. Caius whispered that they were the only ones rich enough to afford cabins.

'My father would pay for me to have a stuffy little coop to sleep in, but I would rather lie in the fresh air under the stars,' he added and Kayin smiled at his enthusiasm.

The Isis set sail as the sun climbed higher in the clear skies and the summer trade winds carried them on a swift northerly course. The helmsman's hand was always on the tiller which guided the long steering oars. Kayin watched the sailors skilfully trimming the big square mainsail and clambering among the webs of rigging, while down on the decks the passengers slept, gossiped and played dice. He did not allow himself to wonder about where he was going, willing his mind to stay dull and blank, dutifully accepting favours but no more.

The weather stayed fair and the nights on deck were pleasantly cool beneath the canopies which Titus erected for them every evening. Caius set himself to teach Kayin Latin and declared himself amazed at how quickly he mastered the rudiments of the language. Sometimes he talked to Kayin about his family—his prosperous, powerful father, his younger brothers, his wife Prisca whom he married when she was only twelve, his mother Antonia and her horde of wealthy friends. Kayin avoided questions about himself and the partner he had lost, and eventually Caius stopped asking. He never seemed to resent Kayin's silence, and his generosity extended to sharing the meals which Titus prepared for him in the ship's galley.

Towards mid-morning on the fifteenth day, the Isis came to the mouth of the Tiber and the sea port of Ostia. The captain made the customary thanksgiving sacrifice on the poop deck and one of the harbour tugs rowed the ship to dock, where the sailors moored her to an enormous stone ring on the quay. As soon as the gangplank was lowered, dockhands swarmed on board to unload the cargo of Egyptian grain, brought across the sea to fill the hungry stomachs of imperial citizens. While the grain was loaded onto barges for towing to the warehouses of Rome, Kayin accompanied Titus and Caius as they hired a mule-drawn carriage for the final stage of their journey.

Caius had already pressed Kayin to spend at least one night at his family home, warning him about Roman inns with lurid tales of cut-throats and bed-bugs. As they bowled along the paved road, he told Kayin that the carriage would take them right to the door of his house.

'We'll arrive long after dark, you see, and it's only then that we can drive into the city itself,' he explained. But the mule-driver made the journey in better time than expected and they were one of the first carriages to enter the streets of Rome. There was just enough light for Kayin to see the palaces and temples, the arches and bridges, all built from cut stone and brick and magnificent above the noisy, littered streets.

At last they halted outside a barred door set in high walls. Before Kayin had climbed down, Titus was at the door, summoning slaves to unload the baggage. Stepping warily into a confusion of shouted greetings, orders and exclamations on the young master's return, he was tempted to disappear quietly into the labyrinth of streets. Then Caius caught his arm and led him over the threshold.

As he entered the house, Kayin heard a girl singing somewhere within. The tune was a little uncertain, but the voice was sweet and clear.

'Surely that is Prisca!' Caius said happily, but Kayin was silent, troubled in heart. Although the girl sang in Latin and he could not understand the words, he knew the sound of them. They were the words he had struggled to understand in the wilderness, spoken by a strangely familiar voice on the edge of hearing.

23

Imperial City

In the flurry of welcomes and introductions, Kayin stood apart, confusedly debating what had happened. What was this calling, this baffling coincidence of voice and song that followed him? Was it drawing him on somewhere? He feared to shape answers to his questions, knowing too surely that whatever corner he turned, wherever he walked, the curse went before him to blight the way. That, at least, was assured and inescapable.

A little of his attention engaged with the talk going on around him as he heard Caius explain who his guest was and why he had come. Women's voices murmured sympathetically at his plight.

'My father, Marius Aemilianus Varro,' said Caius, addressing Kayin in Greek. Kayin acknowledged the tall, austere-looking man who bowed to him. 'He has more power than the rest of the Senate put together if you believe the gossips on street corners. My mother Antonia, who is beautiful by profession.' Kayin smiled at the gracious dark-haired woman who said she was pleased to welcome any friend of her son.

'My youngest brother Claudius,' Caius went on, 'who is cleverer than all of us.' A lad of about thirteen years nodded at Kayin. 'Cornelius who will soon have his sixteenth birthday and coming of age, and Marcus, next in age to me and studying to be the greatest orator since Cicero.' Caius stopped and looked round. 'And my wife?' he said in Latin.

'She is coming now,' said Antonia, but Caius was already talking of something else, pointing across the hall.

'Where has the altar gone? And the household gods?' Kayin noticed that none of the assembled household met his gaze except his father who hesitated and then did not answer his questions.

'Come, dinner is waiting for us and we have a great deal to tell you. Many things have changed in Rome during these past two years.'

Caius seemed about to pursue the matter of the altar further, when somebody else appeared through a curtained doorway, hanging back shyly as she saw the crowd around the new arrivals.

'Prisca!' Caius crossed the floor in three enthusiastic bounds and kissed her on both cheeks. Stepping back, he looked her up and down. 'You've grown taller, haven't you? And your hair—it's fairer than it was?' She nodded, demurely clasping her hands in front of her.

Caius led her to the others. 'Prisca, this is my friend who saved my life in Alexandria. His name is Kayin and he learns Latin almost as fast as you learn Greek. She has more brains than me,' he said to Kayin, 'but she's a good wife. When a girl looks at you as she looks at me, it makes you feel like a god!' Kayin smiled, but the rest of the family appeared uneasy, although until then they had laughed freely at Caius' lively humour.

Antonia broke the awkward silence. 'The servants will take you and your friend to wash and change your clothes after your long journey. We will wait for you before we eat.' She spoke Latin slowly enough for Kayin to understand. He sensed that the family were not altogether pleased about having to entertain an unexpected guest, but when he suggested as much to Caius as they climbed the stairs to the upper rooms, the young man dismissed his fears.

'Nonsense. They've always been hospitable enough. Maybe there's been some trouble with my brothers. My father will explain at dinner.'

After washing and changing into clean tunics, they pulled on the longer, fuller over-tunics customary for the formal business of dinner and went down to the dining-room. The couches stood ready beside the table which was spread with a clean linen cloth. The evident prosperity of the Varro household impressed Kayin as servants entered with platters of food which they offered to each diner in turn, and others came with bowls of water and towels for washing the hands between courses.

Kayin studied Prisca as he ate, while the rest of the family chattered in Latin, often speaking all at once. All except Marius who was as silent as his daughter-in-law. The head of the household was not shy, Kayin suspected, but possessed a kind of lordly reserve, as a lion might sit magnificently apart, watching his offspring at play. Prisca, however, seemed to be a mouse of a girl and Kayin was puzzled as to why Caius should be so devoted to her. Kayin thought her uninteresting and quite ugly, with a wide, colourless face, square chin and undistinguished nose. Her looks faded into insignificance beside Antonia's glowing charms.

Kayin wondered how others saw him. In one of the upper rooms he had glanced in a polished mirror and had been dismayed by the ageing man he saw reflected there. Caius' parents were surely surprised by their son's choice of companion.

My life is running out, he thought wildly, *like sand running through my fingers. But how will it end? Will it ever end?* Realising somebody was speaking his name, he roused himself and tried to look attentively round the semi-circle of couches.

'Kayin.' It was Marius breaking his lion-like silence. 'I must apologise for not offering you finer food. We did not know Caius would bring a guest home with him. Tomorrow we shall hold a more sumptuous affair with musicians and poets and food fit for the emperor's table.'

'But not for me, Father?' Caius asked good-humouredly. 'Didn't I deserve a feast this evening? I thought my return home would be a noisier affair. Are you holding a secret from me? Even Claudius is not as cheerful as I remember.'

Suddenly everybody around the table was quiet. Even the servants stood still, as if expecting the order to leave the room which Marius gave by a nod. Nobody else moved or made a sound.

'We have news for you which we wanted to tell in private,' Marius said carefully. 'The household has changed. We—your mother and myself, your brothers, the whole household—we belong to the Christians now.'

At first speechless, Caius began to laugh, and then checked himself, staring at each of his family in turn.

'When? When and why?' he spluttered. 'Are you joking? No, I see that's not so from your dour faces.' As the others started to reply, interrupting one another's explanations, Kayin took the opportunity to turn to Prisca who was reclining on his right. Indifferent to the matter of what gods the family served, he burned to learn more about the song she had been singing.

'Tell me...' He raised his voice a little and she eyed him anxiously. His grim, scarred face probably frightened her. 'What were you singing when Caius and I arrived?' He asked the question in Latin, brow furrowed with concentration.

She blushed. 'A song of—of the Christians, translated from the Greek. I was at my prayers.'

'And the words you used?' Kayin asked hurriedly, afraid of interruption before he could get to the truth.

'The words—"Sleeper, awake. From your grave arise, for the light of the Anointed One is..." '

'And you, Prisca? You've joined the Christians too?' Caius swept their conversation aside. When Prisca nodded, he shook his head impatiently. 'You realise, don't you, that Christians are unpopular people these days, just as in the past? Haven't you heard about the riots in Alexandria earlier this year?'

'We heard there was trouble,' Marius said.

'Trouble! It was a massacre!' Caius got up from his couch and paced around the table. 'The people turned on the Christians. They looted and burned their property, and dragged them to the temples to sacrifice them to the imperial gods. They beat an old woman to death in the street. Have you thought about your position, Father? The family reputation? Your sons' careers?'

Kayin closed his mind to the quarrel, withdrawing into himself to consider what Prisca had told him. *I do not understand what I have heard,* he thought, *but a voice called me awake in the desert and I shall wait until it calls me again. There is nothing else left for me.*

Later, when dinner and debate were over and the

household had retired to bed, he lay awake on a woollen mattress in the guest chamber. Outside the shuttered window the night traffic rumbled past, carts and carriages rolling in and out of the city. The knowledge grew in his heart that he did not have the strength of will to walk on from Rome. He could not take another forward step in his lifetime of journeying until he heard the call again, so clear he could not doubt it.

An early bell roused the servants to their morning duties and the family rose soon afterwards. Cautiously descending the stairs, Kayin found the entire household gathered in the hall around the central pool of clear water. He joined Caius on the edge of the group.

'They're going to say their prayers,' Caius said in a jeering undertone. 'Look, my father has a book because they don't know the words yet. Fledgling Christians!' Kayin watched as they faced east and Marius read out a brief invocation and what sounded like a series of blessings. The others joined him in speaking prayers of intercession and dedication.

'So devout!' Caius mocked. 'My father has merely replaced old gods with new. And look at my brothers—it's just novelty to them. They'll soon forget it.'

'And Prisca?' Kayin could not help asking.

Caius snorted. 'She disappoints me. I thought she saw things more clearly, but she's as credulous as the stupidest slave-girl.'

When the prayers were over, the servants dispersed to clean the house and prepare for the welcome feast which Marius was giving that evening to celebrate his son's return. Caius himself was summoned to his father's side to greet the procession of clients who called every morning to enjoy the patronage of the house of Varro. The family had only recently returned to the city after spending the hottest of the summer months at one of their country villas, but the queue of humble supplicants was longer than ever, or so one of the servants whispered to Kayin. Word had spread that the eldest son was home and many men were anxious to curry favour with him so that he would continue offering them patronage on inheriting his father's wealth. Kayin observed it all from a corner, as client after client received a small gift of money with profuse thanks, and paid elaborate compliments to Caius who smiled on them benevolently.

As the better-dressed, cleaner clients gave way to a ragtag assortment of unemployed artists and freed slaves, Kayin slipped out into the hall and loitered uneasily by the pool. Although tempted again to abandon his friend and vanish into the city, he considered it wiser to take advantage of the family's welcome while it lasted. A glimpse of Prisca in rustling red silks reminded him once again of the song she had sung and repeated to him at dinner. Should he press her to explain the matter further? Eventually he decided against doing so. Deep within, he believed the calling must come again, and come to him alone. He could not depend on Prisca's words.

At noon Caius rejoined him, and after eating a quick meal of bread and cheese, they set out for the baths accompanied by two slaves.

'Tonight you'll see the true hospitality of my father's table,' Caius said with mock-gravity, 'and it's better to bathe and take exercise before eating, as my tutor in Alexandria always told me.'

While they walked, he talked at length about his family, evidently concerned about their new religion. 'I find it impossible that my father should decide such a thing. He is such a stern man, a true Roman, always condemning the people who are drawn into mystical cults, worshipping the Great Mother or Priapus, shrieking like madmen in the markets. He always refused to watch their processions and festivals and poured scorn on their wild emotion and endless star-gazing. "Depraved," he called them. "Disloyal to the emperor." ' Caius paused for breath. 'And these Christians believe they're the only ones with the truth. How could my father forget his dignity and reputation and join his good name with a bunch of intolerant bigots? It can't last. It must not last.'

Kayin tried not to hear the monologue which bored him. He sensed the hum of the great city around him, the unseen wheels of trade turning at the centre of the world. The streets were so tightly packed that sometimes he could hardly squeeze through, but he did not mind the breathless jostle because of the beauty of the buildings lining the way. Palaces and public buildings standing shoulder to shoulder with the tenements of the poor, some of them faced with marble which reflected the afternoon sun and dazzled the eyes.

All this, said Kayin to himself. *All this prosperity built by men's hands. Men who do not weep over the dust and ruins of old empires.* Hot pride filled him. *One day,* he thought, *they will build a city which will last for ever and no enemy will ever break down its walls.* The dream of his young days came back to him—the wide bright streets and the houses touching the sky—and he knew that not every trace of hope had died within him. He found he was smiling as he passed the stalls of the pastry cooks, the barbers shaving customers before a crowd of onlookers, the money-changers guarding their tables stacked with coins. Beggars whined and clutched at passers-by, fishmongers shouted their wares, and silversmiths, shoemakers and carpenters toiled in cramped workshops.

Caius brought him to the city's newest public baths, the Thermae of Antoninus, where citizens found exercise for both body and mind. Saluting old acquaintances, he took Kayin past the vaulted reservoirs of water, brought to the city by aquaduct, and into a shaded courtyard where groups of young men wrestled in clouds of dust or played at ball around a fountain. Two of the wrestlers untangled themselves to wave to Caius and he embraced them, leaving Kayin staring at the sunlight on the fountain.

It is a city of heroes, he thought, *where men have made homes for living like gods*. He marvelled at the spacious bathing rooms, each modulated to a particular degree of heat or cold, and the mosaic pavements, the play of water in stone basins, the marble statues in every alcove, and everywhere the proud citizens of Rome standing or sitting or lying down and making conversation with their friends.

The next few days went by in the same easy, pleasant way, although Kayin spent less time in Caius' company as the young man renewed friendships and set about making a place for himself in Roman society. On the seventh day, Marius called Kayin for a private interview before the first of his clients arrived. They sat facing one another on stools placed ready by one of the servants who also acted as Marius' secretary.

'You are welcome to stay with us as long as you need,' Marius began, 'but perhaps you could tell me what you propose to do now that you have come to Rome.'

Kayin groaned inwardly, hating such a question. 'I propose nothing.' He met Marius' shrewd eyes and knew the other was wondering why his son was involved with such a strange man.

'I could offer you work if you wanted it. I need somebody to act as overseer on one of my country estates.'

Kayin remembered the feeling of dust—dry, sterile dust—between his fingers. 'You would not want me in charge of your crops. Whatever I touch withers.'

Marius could not know that Kayin was speaking the literal truth, and looked wary. He no doubt thought him a good-for-nothing taking advantage of his son's kind heart. 'Do you have any plans for your future?'

'My future!' Kayin's buried desperation rose up. 'Maybe I would rest easy if I were a slave, obeying orders without having to think.'

'You cannot really wish that. Every man cherishes his freedom.'

Kayin dropped his head in his hands. 'I...have... no...freedom.' His voice was hollow. There was a pause, and then he felt Marius' touch on his bowed shoulders.

'You seem a broken man, heart-sick—and no wonder. You endured a terrible thing, losing your loved ones and everything you owned. Yet a man can always build his life again in the end.'

'I am waiting for a summons,' Kayin said abruptly, trying to stop the man's unwittingly cruel talk. For how could he even think of rebuilding and restoration? 'I do not know when it will come, but I believe it will. Until then...'

'Until then I shall be your patron and grant you free lodging in my house.' Marius got to his feet indicating that the interview was over. 'Take heart, my friend. I trust you will find wholeness and healing soon.'

24

The Old Gods

As autumn settled on the city, Caius spent more and more of his time with the band of friends he had gathered about him. Sometimes he stayed away from home for two or even three days at a stretch, without sending any message to reassure his family as to his whereabouts. He was evidently set upon enjoying himself after the years of disciplined study, but Kayin also suspected that he meant to challenge the household's new-found Christian piety. Caius apparently had some idea of behaving in such a dissolute way that they would be shamed into abandoning their beliefs. One evening he drunkenly confided as much to Kayin who met him lurching home long past midnight.

'People will talk,' he mumbled, leaning on Kayin's shoulder. 'They'll laugh at my father. "His religion doesn't help his poor son," they'll say. He won't stand for laughter. A proud man. Always a true Roman.' Kayin left him weeping sentimental tears in the gutter.

His campaign was futile, however. The family continued their daily prayers, soon without written words to prompt their memories, and they met as often as twice a week to eat a meal with other believers.

Kayin, meanwhile, passed through the house like a

shadow, eating and sleeping little. When the family were in bed, he would slip out by a side door and trudge the streets, unafraid of footpads and thieves. They never threatened him. By day he joined the hordes of idlers in the ways and by-ways of the city. Leaving the house before dawn and returning after dark, he scarcely saw the family and avoided meeting them at dinner if he could. After all, how could he say he spent his time? Walking, endlessly walking in the city. Sometimes he neither ate nor slept for several days, always waiting and listening in his heart for the call that did not come.

The more he saw of Rome, the more he marvelled at the craftsmanship of those who had built it. Yet although it was surely the greatest, the most beautiful of all cities, he paced its streets wearily, unable to rest. Sometimes he choked with despair and would walk faster and faster, trying to empty his mind of the terrible fears crowding it. Then he would start running, hurrying uselessly, nowhere, until he found a measure of calm again.

The weather turned colder and there were rumours of political troubles, whispers of turmoil in the crowds, solemn debate between Marius and Caius at the dinner table. People said the news was bad—the emperor was dead. Killed in a clash with his own military commander at Verona. Weeks and days passed and a new emperor entered Rome and the talk was that he would restore the old disciplines and Roman virtues, working to shore up the crumbling borders of the empire. The Varro household was noisy with argument between father and son as Caius prophesied the downfall of the Christians. The emperor who had looked upon them tolerantly had gone and Marius admitted that the believers were worried by events, although more were being added to their number than ever before.

Kayin penetrated deeper into the heart of Rome, dodging boys racing dogs harnessed to wooden carts on the way to the Circus Maximus. As big as a city in itself, it was here that impatient chariot horses pawed the sparkling track and men staked entire fortunes on the colours of their favourite stable. He sat, puzzled, at the theatre and watched actors rollicking through a crude mime show.

One afternoon he joined the throng in one of the huge amphitheatres. That day he stood sick and silent as men fought with men like wild beasts, and the crowd bayed like a pack of hounds at the kill. When the blood gushed red on the sand, he felt the old nausea returning and fought his way along the packed stands and out into cleaner air. Rain was falling steadily from a flat winter sky and Kayin went to find shelter, not only from the wet but from the horror he had just seen. Coming to the marble porticos of the Campus Martius, he gazed out at a huddle of tombs and temples and pondered the ugliness of the human spirit. Somehow it was more vivid, more shocking, among white pillars and dressed stone than among the walls of dried mud and sun-baked clay in older, forgotten cities.

When the rain stopped, he walked in the greenness of the imperial gardens, open freely to the people of Rome. One late rose clung to a bush and the air was liquid with birdsong. The greenness was beautiful in the heart of the city, but Kayin was beginning to see that even Rome was tainted. The streets stank of human and animal filth, and the poorer citizens were crammed together like rats in a sewer. He walked to the vast Forum where libraries held precious manuscripts and archives; where noblemen disɔensed justice in gilded basilicas. And again he found the aint of greed and cruelty like a whiff of decay. The sunset ight glowed on the brilliantly painted panels of the marɔle column, where an emperor had recorded his military riumphs, and to Kayin it was the colour of blood, a gleaming finger dipped in the wounds of the enemy.

Perhaps, said Kayin to himself, *I should have stayed in the desert, in the pure emptiness of rock and sky.* Perhaps he could return to the hermit in his restful solitude. There he could embrace quiet and forget humankind whose soul-filth broke through everything they did, like a leprous corruption.

And I, he thought, *I alone can see this truth, while the rest of them run crying after little gods, foolishly hoping to be saved from their own sickness. I stand alone and apart, and only my eyes see truly.*

The troubled relations between Caius and his father erupted again as the week-long festival of the Saturnalia drew near—a time of banqueting when patrons loaded their clients with presents of silverware, schools closed for a holiday and everybody, young and old, indulged in gaming, playing dice and knucklebones and exchanging bets.

Talking to Kayin, Caius had described the jollities of the Saturnalia at length, remembering nostalgically the celebrations of his childhood.

'It's the tradition that slaves are never punished during the holiday,' he said. 'They would dine with us in the evening and join in the drinking and jesting afterwards. We'd throw dice to choose a king and then we had to do whatever they ordered, acting like clowns. Once my father had to sing a song, and in the spirit of the Saturnalia he did it willingly. He even danced!' He paused.

'And so?' Kayin could tell that he was leading to another complaint about the new order in the household.

'This year they've chosen to believe the lies of the Christians who whine and complain every year, at every festival, saying that it's evil and pagan.'

The true battle commenced when Caius confronted Marius in the hall and demanded to know why no preparations were underway for the Saturnalia. Marius must have answered shortly that the family would not be celebrating that year, because when Kayin entered the argument was already fierce.

'We'll be shamed and singled out,' Caius was saying angrily, his face red and bloated beside his father's pale, pinched countenance. 'The whole of Rome will laugh at us, at me!'

'For someone so very concerned with the family's good name, as you've declared so many times, you waste your own time in sport and drinking and in idle talk in cookshops and taverns.' Kayin had never seen Marius so roused.

'Pleasure—have you Christians forgotten the word? And simple companionship? Simple delights?'

'Pure self-indulgence. You are ruled by your appetites.'

'And what will you do during the Saturnalia? Fast and wear a sour face and keep the purses tight shut so that children throw stones at our door because of our meanness?'

Kayin edged past before Caius could draw him into the quarrel, but a noisier interruption brought all three of them to a halt. Cornelius, the son next in age to the youngest, rushed into the hallway from the street.

'Father, I heard the news before I reached the schoolmaster's. Everybody's talking about it.' He rested his hands on his knees, trying to catch his breath.

'What news?' asked Marius, alarmed at the boy's urgency.

'The emperor has acted against the church. They've arrested Bishop Fabian and some of the deacons, and they'll put them on trial for bringing harm on the empire and turning the people from the old gods.'

'So,' said Marius after a pause, 'it has started. I did not think it would come yet—not so soon.' He looked suddenly haggard, older. 'It will not be long before all the Christians suffer.' Kayin glanced at Caius, but his friend was expressionless. Sighing as if in unspoken sympathy, Kayin walked on towards the street door, his footsteps very loud in the silent hall. He would leave them to their family rages.

As winter deepened, the news became worse. In the closing days of January, the bishop, leader of the Roman church, was executed, and then even Caius' triumph over his family's distress turned to worry. He had mocked that they would abandon their new beliefs at the first sign of trouble, but instead the Christians were drawing closer together. Little bands of men called on Marius after dark and held earnest discussions behind a closed door, always concluding with one of the believers' wailing hymns. Antonia stayed at home, her face sometimes swollen with tears, but her composure never cracking in front of the family. Of Prisca Kayin saw nothing. It was as if she were in hiding.

One short winter afternoon, Kayin was sitting on a barber's bench in a downtown inn, waiting his turn for the razor to remove three days' growth of stubble from his chin. All around him men debated the state of the empire, the unseasonably mild weather, the price of bread, the petty intrigues of senatorial politics. Suddenly the man on his left addressed him.

'What's your opinion of the new decree, friend?'

'What decree?' Kayin asked.

'Surely you've heard? The emperor's order to make sacrifice. Every man, woman and child must sacrifice to the imperial gods on the prescribed day.'

'How...sacrifice?' Kayin spoke with difficulty as ancient, ineradicable memories crowded his head at the thought of sacrifice.

'Burn a pinch of incense on the altars, pour a libation and taste the sacrificial meats. Nothing fancy. You get a certificate to show you've done your duty.'

'And if you don't sacrifice?'

The man snorted with laughter at Kayin's question. 'If you refuse, then it means death. How can an ordinary citizen think of disobeying an imperial decree?'

'But the Christians, those who call themselves believers? They will not even celebrate the Saturnalia. Surely they...'

'I suppose they can go on worshipping their crucified one in private, so long as they pay public homage to the old gods—to Jupiter, Minerva, Juno, whoever they please.' The man wet his lips with the tip of a pointed tongue. 'I shall sacrifice to Venus,' he said and winked.

For once, Kayin decided to return home before nightfall. The news of the decree made him fear for the family's safety. Of course they would be persuaded to make the necessary public gestures, but he wanted to ensure they knew how matters stood. Hurrying through a maze of short cuts, he came to the house as the servants were lighting the lamps. None of the family seemed to be at home, but just as he was about to go outside again, Prisca appeared in a doorway.

When she saw him, she started retreating into the corridor behind her, but Kayin called for her to wait.

'I have important news for you—for the whole of your family.'

'Yes?' she said timidly, surprised that he should wish to speak to her. He told her the bare outline of the story he had heard from the man at the inn.

When he had finished, she was quite still. Her eyes shone bright and she breathed fast, as if she had a fever.

'Well?' Kayin said, staring at her. 'What will you do?'

'What will I do?' A shiver ran through her body. 'I shall...I shall pray that my faith will survive the crucible unharmed.'

'What do you mean?'

Prisca spoke fast, her gaze fixed above Kayin's head. 'I have asked that my faith would be tested. Now the time has come.'

'You know that disobeying this decree means death?' he asked incredulously.

'Only as you understand death. Whatever happens to our bodies cannot touch our souls. I know I will be purged of sin and impurity—all of us will be. We will be like candles. Pure light shining out.'

25

Loyal Citizens

In the excitement of what she was saying, Prisca appeared to have forgotten that she had ever been afraid of Kayin. 'I've prayed for you. I've seen you watching me and I know you've heard the calling too.'

It was strange how her face was transfigured, almost beautiful, in her passion. Kayin knew at once of whom she reminded him then. Like a throb of pain, he recognised something of Elissa in the Roman girl. She had the same look of absolute devotion; all sense of self absorbed into the creed or god—whatever it was—that she followed. Prisca's eyes, however, held nothing of the watchful presence that had often brooded over the Carthaginian priestess.

Wondering at the change in her, he tried to prolong the conversation. 'What god can ask so much as the death of his followers?'

'It is love, not death,' she replied quickly.

To Kayin's ears she sounded ridiculously young and simple. 'You are scarcely more than a child. How can you talk so easily about such matters? Your life is your very own, a precious thing. Take and hold it for yourself and forget about gods.'

'But what I know is real life. So real that in comparison the everyday world is like death. It is something in my heart—I cannot explain it well.' She faltered and looked up at Kayin, her face an innocent child's face. Kayin could see that there had never been any shadow or blight on her life. Suddenly he was angry and wanted to crush her.

'What can you know about death?' he spat out. 'You say the word so glibly, but a girl like you ought to find other, less dangerous, words to play with.'

'But I know what I have found,' she said earnestly. 'Like you, I was called. It was like waking from sleep, like day coming in my heart.'

'Like waking from sleep,' Kayin repeated, half to himself. He was once again lying beneath the desert sky as the voice sang on the edge of hearing; singing words that Prisca had repeated to him on his first night in Rome.

'I heard a voice,' he said abruptly, watching for her reaction. 'In the desert it called me from sleep. I think it brought me here, but now...'

'Now you are waiting.' Prisca moved closer to him in her eagerness. 'I can see that you're waiting, but you haven't heard anything more yet, have you?'

Kayin did not directly acknowledge the accuracy of what she had said. 'I think...I think we two are perhaps alike. I think we both see certain matters more clearly than other people. Matters to do with kinds of truth, perhaps.' Prisca looked at him doubtfully. 'Already you see that I am different from others. Maybe one day I'll explain it to you, but for now you must trust me and listen to what I have to say. The soul-filth, the evil in men's hearts, is turned on you and your fellow-believers, and it will destroy you unless you hide yourselves.'

'I know about evil in the heart.' Her answer came almost defiantly.

'No, you cannot possibly know the full truth of it. Now this is what you must do...'

Somebody coughed behind them and Kayin turned. Caius was watching them intently.

'Did I disturb you?' he called. 'I found your conversation very interesting. I hope you were persuading my wife to drop her silly beliefs.'

Prisca said nothing, worriedly clenching and unclenching her fists. Kayin was reminded of how he had first seen her, Caius' dowdy wife, too frightened to look a stranger in the eye.

'You must have heard the news,' said Caius. 'The first day of sacrifice is in five days' time.'

'That is something I had not heard.' Kayin tried to cover his confusion with coldness.

'I think we can count on this household not receiving a summons immediately. We will have time to persuade them.'

'So there is no chance that anyone will be overlooked?'

'The authorities will use the census and the tax rolls, so nobody can escape for long—but we'll have a little time.' Caius came to the centre of the hall, hands on hips. 'We'll begin with you, Prisca.' Before he could continue, one of the servants hurried to answer a cautious knock at the street door. As the lamplight spilled into the darkness, Kayin saw a small group of men outside. They were obviously anxious to come in because they entered on the heels of the servant without waiting for Caius to issue a welcome.

Kayin recognised them as some of the family's fellow-believers, as did Caius who greeted them curtly and listened without bothering to conceal his impatience as they asked to await Marius' return.

'You will realise that we must see him tonight,' said the group's spokesman, a skinny man with a mild, sheepish face and sandy hair. 'We hope you'll allow...'

'Yes, yes,' Caius broke in. 'You may wait here. But I'll tell you right now that I mean to speak some sense into this household before the day is finished.'

The sandy-haired man bowed apologetically. 'We are always willing to discuss the truths we believe, but we hope we are not too...'

Caius scowled at the man who shrank among his friends. 'I reject and despise you and your insane ideas, and I'll fight against every shadow of your influence on my family.' At that, Prisca came forward and tried to take her husband's hand, although he shook her off furiously.

'Please!' she cried in a thin voice. 'Please. You must not be so angry with them.'

'What is this disgraceful uproar?' Unnoticed to any of them, Marius had arrived, Antonia beside him. Kayin guessed that they too had hurried home after hearing of the emperor's decree.

Caius started to speak, but Prisca quietly interrupted. 'The brothers came to see you. They must speak with you.'

'I see,' Marius said heavily. 'I think we should sit together and discuss the matter in an orderly fashion.' He nodded at the servant who led them from the hall into a side room and brought extra stools to seat the guests.

'I hope you won't waste your time listening to every word of these fellows,' Caius started contemptuously. Marius silenced him with a glare.

'Forgive my son's hot temper,' he said to the guests who coughed and shifted on their stools.

'Maybe,' the sandy-haired man mumbled, 'maybe matters are not as simple as your son thinks.'

'Explain.' Marius leaned towards him.

The man clutched at the folds of his toga. 'This decree, the emperor's decree...'

One of his companions, quivering with tension, burst out, 'None of us can escape. They have our names, and whoever does not appear will be executed.'

'What are you proposing?' Marius asked.

Quite unexpectedly Antonia broke down into noisy tears. The others sat open-mouthed until she grew calm enough to speak.

'This whole business, this Christianity, is too much.' Struggling to control her sobs, she went on, 'I've suffered enough already, cut off from my friends, my closest, lifelong friends. And I suppose you want to throw away everything else—your family's good name, your possessions, your citizenship—all gone when just a little veiling of the truth would save us.' Her words dissolved into weeping and Caius jumped up, knocking over his stool and went to stand at his mother's side.

'Well?' he said aggressively. 'You hear what she says. Should this good Roman woman be dragged to court, tortured and sentenced, perhaps sent into exile, perhaps put to death? You Christians daydream about dying like heroes in the amphitheatre, but have you thought how it would really be? Think of this good, kind woman nailed to a gibbet in front of a howling mob, or whipped until her blood covers the pavement. You disgust me!'

One of the other Christians, one who had not yet spoken, raised his hand as if asking permission to open his mouth. 'Excuse me, but the young man is right. We face terrible consequences and it isn't only the courts we fear. I hear that in Alexandria ordinary men and women set upon believers in the streets and almost beat them to death for treason.'

Marius sat with head bowed and eyes closed, and Kayin wondered if he was praying.

'So what do you advise?' he asked without opening his eyes. 'What do you, my fellow-believers, think is right for us?' He sounded like a defeated man.

The sandy-haired spokesman put on an ingratiating smile. 'These days are not the old days of the first martyrs. The church has grown so strong that it would be madness to break it and lose our leaders and our influence.' His eyes flickered around the room. 'We feel it would be best to preserve our strength; to go along with this petty decree and wait until the storm dies down. And it will die, soon.' There was a weighty silence. A pair of flies circled above their heads in endless, buzzing circles.

At last Marius spoke. 'I think,' he cleared his throat, 'that you are right. My family will follow your example.'

Caius turned triumphantly to Kayin. 'Reason conquers passion! Isn't that so? I knew we would win them round.' Next to him, Kayin saw Prisca, mute and desperate, her cheeks chalk-white. He knew she was waiting for him to speak, to save her.

'Everyone should be faithful to what their heart tells them.' The words were meaningless clods of sound in his mouth. Suddenly he was tired. So tired that his head swam. Stumbling from the room, he climbed the stairs to his own small chamber where he hurled himself onto the couch. Lying there, he heard the strains of a hymn floating up from the room where the believers were gathered, and for some reason rage bubbled up inside him. Then the rage became grief for what had happened—for what would happen—to Prisca.

Unfamiliar tears drenched his face as he thought about her, seeing her truly for the first time. He saw how cruelly he had misunderstood her. She had no beauty to win her favour and she could not plead her case eloquently. She would be misjudged, her keenest desires thwarted, and she would begin to know some of the pain that blighted his own life.

Already she had looked to him for help down in the crowded room, and he had failed her. From now on, though, he would help her in whatever way he could. He could sense in her something of his own resilient spirit, and although he felt nothing like love for her, he could not bear to think of her wasting herself, enslaved to a false creed among weak-willed people. None of them was worthy of the sacrifices she was strong enough to make.

His mind ran on as he lay on the couch. He had found hope of companionship again. He was not utterly alone. Maybe they would leave the corrupt city behind, travelling somewhere together. Not as lovers but as faithful friends, brother and sister. As he relaxed into sleep, his mind's eye saw them walking through a dark valley, hand in hand like children.

Later, in the deep night, he moved into a dream like his youthful dream of a city. The shining walls rose on the hill-top and he could hear clear voices singing, although he was still some way off. Somebody was walking at his side; somebody he thought was Prisca, but her face seemed lovely to him and she was laughing and talking as eagerly as his lost priestess had done. As the vision faded and he woke in darkness, he smiled and the memory of the dream was warm inside him.

26

Love and Death

The first day of sacrifice came and went without the Varro household being summoned to the Capitol where the temple of Jupiter stood, hallowed to the father of all the gods. Another day was decreed, falling exactly two weeks later, and in the intervening time many Christians flocked to Rome. They brought word that the persecutions were fiercer elsewhere and that very many believers—some said vast numbers—were giving way and obeying the imperial orders. Even leaders of the church.

The family turned the force of their guilt and fear on Prisca who still refused to consider concealing her faith. Even though she did not condemn them for their betrayal, they treated her as if she had. Kayin saw her flinch under Marius' cold anger and Caius' mockery, but she did not yield.

'Are you deaf?' Marius asked her. 'Do you not hear the news from Carthage, from Alexandria? All believers are choosing a reasonable course and using a little deception to save the church from great hardship. If you insist on standing alone, you will simply look foolish, a foolish girl.'

'Not quite all,' said Prisca almost inaudibly.

'Speak up!' Caius snapped.

'There are some who resisted here in Rome.' Prisca looked down as she spoke. 'They were arrested.'

'How do you know?' demanded Marius.

'I've been visiting them in prison.' A new storm broke over Prisca's head as she made this confession. Kayin could not bear to witness any more, so he went out to walk the streets, wondering when the right moment would come for him to step in and save her from them.

To his surprise, Caius came to him the very next morning, asking if he could help to persuade his wife. 'I never knew her will was so strong. We've pleaded with her, argued with her, coaxed her and ordered her to follow the rest of the household, but she won't.'

'So what can I do?' Kayin asked.

'Flatter her, threaten her—whatever you want.' Caius heaved a sigh. 'I am going to try other ways. Maybe I can find somebody to forge a certificate of sacrifice or bribe the magistrates.'

'How long do I have?'

'Not long. My father is a prominent citizen and our absence on the first sacrificial day was noticed. Questions were asked. Of course everyone knows he is one of the believers and they're waiting to see what he will do.'

Kayin escorted Prisca to one of the imperial gardens and they walked among the leafless trees as the winter sun gilded an oval pool of shallow water. He painted her a grim picture of imprisonment, torture and shameful death in front of thousands in the arena.

'And for what?' he finished. 'For a few odd beliefs that a handful of men dreamed up no more than a couple of lifetimes ago. Prisca, you are a fine, proud girl. Do not waste yourself over this affair. Save yourself and then I can teach you what I know about love and death and truth.'

'I am not afraid.' She did not try to counter any of his arguments, but simply refused persuasion, standing quietly beside him in her blue woollen cloak. 'Of course it's hard when you all turn on me, but you must not think I'm afraid of you—any of you.'

'Do you not fear pain? Torture?'

'Although my body weakens at the thought of it, my heart is strong. Every day that passes brings me a little more strength. I cannot give in now!' She glanced across at him. 'What will you do?'

'My name is not recorded on any list or census. I came to Rome out of the wilderness and I can escape back there whenever I choose.'

'Will you go soon?'

'Prisca, you could come with me. We still have time to slip out of the city. We could go north, find somewhere safe where nobody would force you to follow their way. You would be free.'

'But I would not be,' she countered. 'I would never be free of the shame, remembering how I failed at the end. And how could I leave my husband and my family?'

How could they still mean anything to you? Kayin wanted to ask, but did not. He saw that the determined spirit he admired was set immovably against him.

As the days went by, there were rumours of a new flowering of hatred against the Christians—stories of tombs being ransacked and believers' bodies taken out and cut in pieces and thrown to the dogs. Mobs prowled certain quarters of the city, breaking into Christian homes and stealing anything of value before dragging out the furniture and burning it in the road. Prisca remained unmoved. Caius' efforts at bribery came to nothing, as did his plans to forge a certificate of sacrifice. The sandy-haired believer visited the house to speak to Prisca, waving his own certificate and trying to persuade her that he had done nothing wrong by complying with the emperor's will. When she would not listen, he grew so querulous that Caius lost his temper and threw him out of the house.

The household rose early on the day of sacrifice and prepared silently for the walk to the Temple of Jupiter Capitolinus where the ceremonies were taking place. They did not sing any hymns or pray together—nor had they done so for almost a week. Kayin suspected that none of them, not even the humblest servant, could act without a crushing sense of shame. At the third hour they all set out for the Capitol.

'Of course we may not be able to sacrifice today,' said Caius to Kayin in conspiratorial tones. 'There may be such crowds that the ceremonies will have to be prolonged over two days.'

Many other people were walking in the same direction and soon Marius' household was absorbed in a greater procession. The general mood was one of laughter and holiday, with friends yelling greetings to one another and passing comments on others they saw in the throng.

'Look! Marius the Christian and the holy family,' jeered one voice, and people turned to stare. Marius carried on with impeccable dignity, paying no attention to the cries of mockery that followed his progress. Failing to catch Prisca's eye, Kayin gradually withdrew into the crowd, intending to watch at a distance. If she was arrested for refusing to sacrifice, he was sure her family would disown her. Then he would go to her in prison, when she was frightened and alone, and bring her out.

And then, he said to himself, *we will be together and I will not have to journey alone. At least not for a while.*

Ahead of him he could see the family arriving at the temple where worshippers and temple officials were milling about and the tribunals sat dispensing certificates to those who had fulfilled their duties. From time to time the noise and bustle intensified as one of the gangs of vigilantes dragged an unwilling man or woman to the altars, while onlookers hooted with laughter. Others were making a big show of hurrying up, almost panting to get at the sacrificial meats.

'They're the ones who are afraid,' said a man to Kayin. 'Almost sure to be Christians and hoping to hide it.'

'And those?' Kayin pointed to five pallid men who were being guarded by soldiers. Several had limbs tied in stained bandages or some other mark of injury about them.

'Those?' The man jerked his thumb at the men disparagingly. 'They've had their spirits broken in prison and they've come to make a public show of their loyalty to the emperor. It sometimes takes a lot of pain to break them.'

Marius was gravely walking forward, his family behind him, neither holding back nor rushing up the broad marble steps. People drew aside respectfully to let him through, and the hubbub lessened so that Kayin heard the senator's name read out by one of the officials, calling him and his household to sacrifice. Above the crowds of worshippers were ranged many statues of the Roman gods, blank-eyed, bloodless deities standing watch over the people. Kayin started to push to the front of the crush, trying to see Prisca.

'I am a Christian.' Her voice reached him through a

sudden lull. 'I will not sacrifice.' Suddenly he was standing in the open, perhaps six feet from where Prisca faced the temple official, who was a fat man with pouchy, pock-marked features.

'Take my advice, girl, and obey the emperor's orders. Follow your family's example and stop this game,' he said sternly.

'No, I will not.' Prisca's back straightened with determination. Kayin felt her gaining courage with every breath.

The official wagged a plump finger at her. 'Think of what you're saying, girl. If you don't change your mind and sacrifice, you'll be hauled off to prison, and you'll soon lose your pretty looks there. All you need to do is burn a pinch of incense.'

'No.' Prisca was resolute, the flame of her spirit unwavering. Kayin wept for her in his heart.

'You heard that!' Caius spun round. 'Treason on the Capitol, the heart of the empire!' Kayin hardly recognised him, so distorted was his face by impotent rage at Prisca's rebellion. All his affection for her seemed to have turned to hate.

'Very well then.' The official's manner was calm to the point of boredom. 'Arrest her.'

Immediately three temple guards moved from his side to surround Prisca. Caius saw Kayin across the marble pavement and started shouting something, but Kayin pushed away into the crowd without waiting to listen, running from the Capitol.

He did not see the rest of the family again. For the next three days he wandered the city, tracing the network of short cuts and back-alleys which he had discovered at one time or another. Returning at daybreak to the street where

Marius' house stood, he found one of the servants setting off to market and bribed her for information. As he had suspected, the family had cut themselves off from Prisca after her arrest, fearing for their own safety.

'That's not to say they might not come round to visiting the poor girl in gaol,' the servant said, 'but they have to be careful, see?' Kayin pressed her for directions to the prison and set oft at once, only pausing to buy two loaves of bread with some of the coins which Marius had given him at their last meeting as client and patron. The servant told him that what Prisca lacked above all was money for a lawyer to plead her case in court. Kayin had other plans for her.

The turnkey guarding the prison door took most of his remaining coins before letting him in at such an early hour. Another guard was assigned to take him down a stinking passage and into a long, dark room where a rustling of straw and chink of metal chains told him that the prisoners were beginning to wake.

'Where is she?' The guard prodded a heap of rags and a ghastly white face snarled up at them. 'Not this one.'

'Perhaps she is not here.' Kayin looked hurriedly around the crowded chamber. In the poor light it was hard to distinguish the age and sex of any of the sleepers.

'That's her—over there.' The guard pointed to the far corner and Kayin saw Prisca raise her head wearily.

'Kayin!' She was on her feet as soon as she saw him, brushing the straw from her clothes and making a pitiful show of patting her hair into place. He went over and took her in his arms and felt her struggling to control her sobs.

'All is well,' he murmured. 'I have come to take you away. Here, eat some of this.' Breaking off a corner of the warm bread, he handed it to her, but she shook her head.

'Thank you for bringing this to me, but I can't eat it. We're fasting now. Fasting and praying. I know others who will be glad of bread, though.'

'Are you saying there are other believers here?'

Prisca wiped her eyes, composing herself. 'My Christian brothers and sisters. Some of them are in chains. We number fourteen at the moment and we are strong in fellowship together.'

Kayin groaned inwardly. He had assumed she would be alone, friendless and frightened in some airless hole of a cell. Not surrounded by people as misguidedly fervent as she.

'And other believers visit us,' Prisca was saying. 'They are upholding us with their prayers. That girl over there, Sabina, is giving birth soon and we are praying that...'

'Prisca,' Kayin did not let her finish, 'we must leave. I have just enough money to bribe our way out of here, but time is very short.'

'Where are we going?'

'Out of the city. Away to where you will be safe. We shall escape somehow.'

'No.' She stepped back out of his grasp.

'Prisca, you do not know what you are saying. Are you choosing pain and prison and death instead of freedom? For what purpose?'

'I cannot go. I cannot deny my Lord God. Sometimes I do fear—' she bit her lip—'I fear the pain that my body will feel, but I can't be false to what I know is true. And I would be betraying the others here. They need me.'

'Have you thought how much I might need you?' As Kayin asked, he saw a flicker of doubt cross her face.

Then she took hold of his hands. 'Last night I saw a vision as I prayed. I saw you walking alone, going out into the dark, and ahead of you stretched a path like gold. Do you remember the calling you heard? I think this is the answer you were seeking.'

'What do you mean?' Kayin clutched her hands like a drowning man.

'You must go out of the city alone, a pilgrim seeking the truth. The path will open at your feet and you must follow it faithfully.'

'You do not know what I am. I am accursed. Whatever I touch withers.'

'Believe me! You must believe me!' Prisca sounded tearful again and Kayin noticed another older woman prisoner coming towards them, her arms extending in compassion to the girl. He was losing her to the Christians.

'I have to go,' he said to her. 'I cannot stay and watch you suffering. I have seen too much suffering. More than anyone else could bear. But Prisca, you are breaking my heart, what little there is left.'

She kissed him on both cheeks. 'I give you the kiss of peace and of farewell. Trust that the path is there and you will find it. As for me, my place is here. The Lord God be with you and watch over your footsteps.'

As the winter morning came grudgingly to the city streets, Kayin left Rome behind him. The paved road was cold beneath his feet and his heart froze with loneliness, but in his despair he remembered the vision that Prisca had described to him. To honour it was the only act of love he could do for her. She had denied him everything else.

So I will be a pilgrim, he said to himself, *although I do not know where I am going or what it is I seek.* And he walked on.

27

Into the Cold

'How much of the day is gone?' The old pilgrim raised himself on shaking arms to look across at me. I got to my feet stretching my stiff limbs, and stepped outside. A cold wind hissed between the boulders standing sentinel near the cell and down below, at the foot of the cliff, the sea boomed over the great slabs of rock piled there. Above me the sun was already sinking into a mass of thick cloud.

Shivering in spite of my woollen habit, I tried to gather my wits and pray for the old storyteller, but my thoughts seethed as distractedly as an angry swarm of bees. Already I felt changed by what I had heard, my innocence about man and God shattered, and I knew I could not bear to hear much more. Lifting my hands to heaven, I offered our Lord a wordless, desperate invocation before returning to the gloom of the cell.

'My father,' I ventured, 'is your tale nearly done?'

'Wilt thou not hear me out?' He looked at me from under his lids. 'Art thou afraid, boy?'

'Yes,' I said simply.

'And dost thou think I had no fear?'

I caught my breath. 'You say now that this truly happened to you? How could...'

He seemed not to hear me. 'Thou wilt have to hold thy peace until I am done. That is the bargain I make with thee. Questions—if thou hast any questions left—come at the end when I have no more to say.' And he took up the thread of the story just as before.

Kayin followed the roads leading straight and true from the city, trudging in the mud with the farm carts and peasants while companies of soldiers and shining chariots travelled swiftly along the paved way. After a few days he stopped noticing the milestones and watched the motion of his feet as they strode onwards, one overtaking the other in ceaseless repetition. Taking the part of a beggar among the people he encountered, he accepted without shame the crusts and scraps of meat they threw to him from tavern doors.

After a time he left the imperial roadways behind, keeping away from human dwellings and climbing up and over the mountains, and then plunging into the beginnings of the great northern forests. He had no way to lose in the greenwood so he wandered in whatever direction his feet took him, through league after league of oak trees and arching groves of beeches. Sometimes the branches were winter bare, and then the summer sun would cast green shadows on the forest floor. At other times the withered leaves floated down onto his grey head. Footstep after footstep, onwards under a pale northern sky—and as he walked, he sensed time dragging at his heels, weighing him down and sapping the last of his strength. His body was growing old and worn out, and he felt weaker with every day that passed.

As he walked through the maze of trees, he listened to the silence underlying the sounds of leaf and twig and footfall. He listened until his ears rang with the emptiness. No voice ever called out to him. Not even in his dreams.

Occasionally he came to clearings in the forest where there was a farmstead with a few fields of grain and pasture and a terrace of vines. More rarely he saw settlements at a ford or a crumbling hill-top fort, but he always kept at a distance unless the barren winter months drove him to beg or thieve on the outskirts. In those short encounters, exchanging a few mumbled words with the frightened peasants, he gathered rumours of a terror from the east; a worse threat than the ancient fight against wolves and wild boar and the darkness beneath the encroaching trees. People feared the coming of barbarians, black-haired devils who rode wild horses and fired arrows from the saddle with unnatural accuracy. The old, familiar world was crumbling at the edges and nobody knew what the end might be.

Kayin slipped through the forest more stealthily than any outlaw band stalking lonely travellers. He carried his own fear with him and when he found men and women lying slaughtered by the ruins of their village, the fear rose within him and made him shudder. But it was not fear for his own skin, because in all his wanderings no man or woman had ever done him bodily harm. It was the hot, salty smell of the blood that sickened him and made him tremble.

One day, when bare branches etched delicate lines against a flat white sky, Kayin was striding on, stamping his feet in the frosty cold. Then unexpectedly, shockingly, the forest silence was disturbed. He heard the thud of hooves. Horses—maybe half a dozen of them. A moment later they came into view, and mounted on their backs were men; young men with white skins, blue eyes and scanty beards. Noticing Kayin at once, they reined in their mounts and came to surround him.

As they shouted at him in their barbarian tongue and prodded him with the butts of their spears, he waited dully to see what they would do. They were dressed strangely to his eyes in tunics of brightly coloured wool, ankle-length breeches and furred cloaks fastened on the shoulder with ornamented gold brooches. One young man in a diamond-patterned tunic wore gold armlets and two fine rings and it was he who shouted loudest, evidently giving orders to the others, because they took Kayin, bound him tightly and flung him over the saddle of one of the horses before setting off at a canter.

Even before he could understand their speech, Kayin guessed that his captors were returning home after a hunting trip or raiding party. He was probably now a slave, seized as their property on the whim of the chieftain's son whose gold rings glittered in the sunshine. For four days they rode north until Kayin was stupified with cold and exhaustion. On the evening of the fourth day they came to a cluster of thatched roofs guarded by a ditch and a fence with a single gateway in the middle. Rough hands jerked Kayin off his horse and into a circle of white barbarian faces. Dimly, he saw his young master arguing with an older man who must have been his father. He did not look impressed with his son's choice of booty.

It was a harsh winter that Kayin spent at the barbarian village. The people lived in houses of wood, mud and straw at the edge of the salt marshes, and the sea-tides boomed in the distance, night and day. For a few days they all glared at him suspiciously and the children ran away screaming whenever they saw him near, but before long they treated him with as little concern as the cattle whose stabling he shared in a musty barn.

'It has always been winter,' he mumbled to himself in the long nights, pressing against the flanks of the animals for warmth. He could remember nothing except the wet, miserable cold and the raw wind that came over the marshes and bit to the marrow.

Although he was as grey-haired and worn as the chieftain, he became the village slave because he was still strong enough to feed the cattle, chop the firewood and draw water from the well. Moreover the chieftain's son, favoured as the only boy among five daughters, treated Kayin as his personal property whenever he wanted someone waiting on him at table. The winter was the time when the fields lay fallow and the men went hunting, and sometimes raiding other settlements, so that the whole clan could gather in the chieftain's hall at nightfall for a feast. Kayin would fill the men's drinking horns from a heavy jar of mead and then go to sit among the broken pottery and bones on the floor, listening to the stories they told. He never mastered enough of their speech to venture his own stories.

From time to time the chieftain would push back his bench and address his people. Sitting in the smoke-filled twilight, Kayin soon knew his words by heart.

'This land is too small for us,' he would begin. 'Soon we must sail away.' He spread his arms wide. 'When the wild geese leave the marshes and fly north, when spring comes, then we will fly too.' He turned to the women sitting with their spindles at one end of the hall. 'We will win ourselves wider lands with rich fields and gold in the streams.' The chieftain's wife would nod, fingering her necklace of glass beads and smiling to herself.

As the darkest days of winter went by, Kayin realised that the villagers meant to leave that very spring, not at some vague future time. He was forced to help the men slaughter most of the cattle—a task that revolted him—and afterwards preserve the meat with salt. The women baked mounds of unleavened barley bread and carefully stored it in sacks, while the children carried firewood and water pitchers. Even the village dogs seemed to notice a change in the air, barking at every shadow and chasing their tails.

Kayin never questioned that he would go too, wherever the villagers were going. He found it restful to think that he had no choices left now that he was a slave bound to his masters and carried along by their strong destiny. When the sailing time came in the spring, they would go to join their kin in a village further up the coast and the young men would lend their strength to their cousins' warrior-band.

Waking at his usual hour one morning, Kayin noticed that the sun was already above the horizon. The time of winter darkness was coming to an end at last and out on the marshes the wild geese were calling to one another, gathering for the long flight north. A rattling at the door latch roused him from his straw couch as his young master, the chieftain's son, entered in a gust of fresh air.

'I have come to give you your freedom.' He did not look directly at Kayin when he addressed him, but let his gaze wander around the barn. 'Today we leave.'

'We go today?' Kayin asked, his spirits quickening with anticipation.

'Not you,' the chieftain's son said abruptly. 'You are free to go away, just as we are going away to our kin for the journey over the sea.' For the space of a breath, Kayin did not understand. Then he felt as if a gulf opened at his feet.

'No—no,' he stammered. 'Do not leave me behind.'

'Leave you? We are turning you loose to be a free man again.'

'But I have nowhere to go. I cannot bear...'

For the first time, the young man looked him in the eyes. It was a look of contempt. 'So my father was right when he called you an old, broken creature. A spirit as wretched as yours does not deserve to live.' He folded his arms. 'We have no room for your kind on our ships, so go. Crawl back to the forest where we found you.'

I thought I had nothing, Kayin said silently. *I thought I had nothing, but I see now there was still something more to be taken from me. I had too much hope.* Once again he felt the weight of his curse upon him, crushing him into the dirt and dung on the barn floor.

Later, the young men of the village came and found him still lying in the barn, so they drove him out with their spears. Clutching the tatters of his cloak around him, he remained standing where they left him, watching as the villagers prepared to leave their homes. Shortly after noon they set off in procession. First came the men armed as warriors with shield and spear. The chieftain carried his sword and iron helmet with its boar crest cast in shining bronze. The women and children followed, driving the few remaining cattle which were laden with baggage. Kayin watched until they vanished from sight. He was left alone save for the wild geese still wheeling and crying over the grey marshes.

A thought came to him that he was free to walk to the sea margin now since he had no wish to stay among the abandoned huts or return to the forest. The only idea he could grasp clearly was that of lingering on the shore, perhaps until he saw the ships sailing from their hidden harbour along the coast. He could not form any other purpose.

As he set out for the shore, the sun was sinking from the midpoint of the spring sky and he found a way across the marsh easily enough. As he continued, however, he found that the world was darkening, as if night was falling early or his eyesight was failing. When he looked to the sky, the sun had vanished. It was hidden behind a black canopy and a dark fog was gathering above him and around him. Yet nothing could move him to fear now—nor indeed to any other kind of emotion—so he carried on walking.

After a time he must have come near the sea because he heard the slap of waves and sometimes felt spray on his cheeks. The ground turned from mud to pebbles and then to sand, and then to pebbles again, but the darkness was growing so thick that before long he had to guess where to place his next step.

After a long time of walking, the thought came to him that the sound of the waves was always on his right hand, drawing closer and then receding far away, and he took some slight comfort from knowing that he was following some direction. After an even longer time, the dark fog started to lighten by slow degrees until at last he saw that he was crossing a curve of sandy beach. The fog gradually dissolved to a clammy white mist, still shrouding all that lay more than a few feet away.

Although Kayin slowed his stride, he did not stop and rest, even after such a time of walking.

'Why should I rest any more?' he asked aloud. 'I am not tired. My body does not ache. No, I must journey, as I have always done.' And as he watched his feet imprinting the smooth yellow sand, he thought about the countless miles he had travelled, the countless years of travelling. In the calm whiteness of the mist he looked back into his past, and for the first time he saw clearly, right to the very beginning. He saw how his fortunes had grown great and dwindled to less than nothing.

'I was like a king once,' he said aloud, 'and I was a potter. I ruled people and I gave my love to one single woman. I saw the moon set over Nineveh and stood at dawn among the tombs of the pharaohs.' Slowly, trying to recall the very taste and smell and touch of his memories, he set about shaping a story in his heart: the story of his days.

Before the story was half-told, he rounded a headland which appeared suddenly out of the mist. Beyond it was another wide stretch of shore. This time, though, the sands were not empty. No more than a few paces away, he saw the bright flames of a woodfire and beside it, holding bare hands to the glow, knelt a hooded figure.

28

At the End

As Kayin approached, the figure rose quickly, pulling back the hood to reveal the face of a young man, maybe thirty years old. He had the brown, weathered skin of one who spent much time out of doors, even in foul weather, and he wore a thick woollen cloak woven in brightly coloured stripes. Beside him on the sand lay a traveller's staff and leather satchel. Although he looked startled when Kayin first appeared out of the mist, he did not challenge him, but simply made room for him to warm himself at the fire. Kayin sat down cautiously and spread his hands to the flames, covertly scrutinising the other man.

'Have you come far?' the man asked eventually, addressing him in heavily accented Latin. Kayin nodded, suddenly too tired to laugh at such a question. *If I answered him truthfully,* he said in his heart, *this man would think me the greatest liar who ever walked the earth.* For a long time they sat side by side in silence, watching the dancing orange flames.

'My name is Patricius,' said the man turning back towards Kayin. He spoke with curious authority and confidence, as if nothing on earth or in heaven would daunt his spirit. Kayin hung his head and said nothing.

‘I won’t ask for your story if you don’t want to tell it,’ Patricius went on. ‘But…’ and he spoke more gently, ‘I can see by your face that you carry a heavy load of pain.’

‘You would not understand what I would tell,’ Kayin muttered.

‘If your heart is troubled by sin, you can make confession to me. I am a man of God.’

Kayin said through clenched teeth, ‘And I—I am a man under a curse.’ The flames danced and the waves washed the shoreline, creeping closer to the tidemark of dried seaweed and smooth pebbles.

‘Accursed?’ Patricius looked at him thoughtfully. ‘So who cursed you and why?’

Kayin reached back into the far past. ‘I did a very great wrong once, many years ago, and I have paid for it over and over again, more times than I can remember.’

‘And what was this great wrong that you did?’

A black cloud of fear engulfed Kayin as the words of the question beat inside his head. How could he tell the truth and see the young man recoil from him? How could he tell what he had kept hidden for so long?

Then a strange thing happened. It was as if the cloud of fear burst and the rain was the tears on his cheeks, and he could not restrain himself any longer. ‘I killed my brother.’

The words disappeared into the misty air and slowly the storm died away. Kayin raised his eyes and met the gaze of Patricius and saw loving pity, not hatred or disgust.

‘Now do you not despise me?’ he asked, steeling himself for the answer.

Patricius shook his head, his loving eyes fixed on Kayin all the while. ‘Do you repent of what you did?’

Kayin withdrew into his thoughts, recalling the very beginning of his story. He saw his brother Hevel standing before him, broad shouldered and strong, smiling down at him with a child's open-hearted smile.

'If he came to me now...' He stopped, realising for the first time that he had never thought of the sting of anger that poisoned his heart in those distant days. As he recalled it now, he felt that he was beginning to understand something; some true thing. 'If he came to me now,' he began again, 'I would embrace him and ask his forgiveness. You see, I never loved him as he loved me.' He stopped, surprised by what he had admitted to a stranger.

'My friend,' Patricius held his hand towards him, palm outstretched. 'Who put the curse on you?'

'I know Him as the one God, El.'

'Can you be sure of that?' Patricius said after a momentary hesitation, and Kayin marvelled at his calm acceptance of what he heard.

Lifting a finger, he pointed to the scar puckering the side of his face. 'Do you not see how I bear His mark?'

Patricius looked where Kayin pointed and then spoke half to himself. 'This is a hard matter.'

'So drive me away now that you know my secret,' Kayin burst out angrily. 'Stone me if that is what you wish. Do not try to hide your contempt.'

'I will not drive you away,' Patricius said quickly.

They sat in silence again and Kayin began to find the presence of the young man as comforting as the warmth of the fire. *There is much goodness in him,* he said to himself. And he looked at Patricius and thought him beautiful, with the beauty of sunlight through a blade of grass; of white clouds in a high wind; of a wild deer running through a forest.

While they sat there, a sea breeze was scattering the mist until the first watery rays of the sun touched sand and wave. Patricius opened his satchel and brought out a loaf of bread and a waterskin.

When Kayin refused his offer of food and drink, the young man reproached him, telling him not to be afraid of accepting a gift freely offered. Kayin did not reply. He could think of nothing to say.

As Kayin broke his fast, Patricius talked of how as a boy he was kidnapped by sea raiders and sold into slavery in a foreign land. 'I had to herd cattle on the lonely hills of that country, on the western rim of the world, but I also learned to pray there. One day the Lord God answered my prayers and I escaped on a ship. Now, after many hard lessons, I'm going home to Britannia, my own land where my father and mother may still be waiting for me. But before long I'll go back to that far, foreign land and preach the words burning in my heart.' He leaned forward to stir the embers of the fire. 'You found me resting here on the shore, contemplating God's mercy before setting off on the voyage home.' He spoke further, touching on matters which Kayin later forgot as his memory grew ever more worn and tired.

When he had eaten the bread and drunk most of the water, Patricius gripped Kayin's hand. 'You haven't finished your confession. I can't absolve you till the end.' Kayin shrugged wearily. 'But will you come with me?' the young man continued. 'We can talk further as we go. I think we have many things to say to one another.'

Kayin found his tongue. 'I am too old. I would hold you back.'

'I won't press you to come.' Patricius got to his feet, gathering his belongings. 'But if you change your mind and follow after me, remember that my path is leading me to the furthest west; to the islands at the end of the earth, as men call them. As you journey, you'll see them first like clouds behind the setting sun.'

The old pilgrim sighed. 'He was a kind-hearted man. When he left, he pulled the cloak from his back and made me take it, because my own clothes were too threadbare for the cold northern nights.'

I trembled where I sat. 'You say that...'

'I took it from him because he gave it with love.' The old man was oblivious to my confusion. 'I watched him walk away. He told me at the end that my path would become clear, as his had, if only I walked on faithfully. When he had gone, I sat on the shore, a cold husk of a man, crying like an orphaned boy because I had found a friend and lost him so soon. I decided then to follow after him, and I did so, step by weary step. My strength was vanishing like smoke as I went. Sometimes the dark fog came around me once more, but it could not blot out my will. I fixed my eyes on the ground and made my feet carry me on.

'I crossed the land of Britannia, past the crumbling, ruinous cities and the straight roads leading nowhere. I saw cattle stabled in tiled villas, bushes thrusting through cracked marble pavements, and broken cisterns and dry fountains. I heard ignorant people describe the great temples and archways as the works of ancient giants, and I knew I was truly near the ends of the earth in that wretched, fearful land. Many others were fleeing west, burying their treasure in the fields and running from the barbarian warriors. Sometimes they took pity on a feeble old man and let me find a seat in their wagons, and my spirit softened, learning to be glad of such simple, kindly deeds.

'No harm came to me as I went west and west again, although I saw warriors fighting each other like dogs, hacking down their enemies and smearing their own faces with the blood. And at the very last, step by weary step, I came here to Arainn like driftwood, to the very end.'

I gazed at him, speechless.

'And did he come here?'

The old man fixed me with his blazing eyes. 'He spoke of the western islands, and when I heard of your community, the brothers living in the west, I knew it must be here. My heart is eased by telling my tale and now I want to speak with him again. Send for Patricius.'

'There...there is nobody of that name here,' I faltered. 'We come from Arainn, not from any far country. Some of the older brothers used to live in Abbot Enda's community on the east side. They are good and holy men, but none has that name.'

The old man, Kayin, lay very still.

'I am accursed.' His voice came like a whisper from a tomb. 'Time slips through my fingers like water. I thought I would find him here, but I am defeated at the very end.' Wrenching one hand free from the coverlet, he shook his fist at the roof of the cell. 'Curse You, El. Curse You. Your arm is indeed long.'

'I will call the other brothers,' I gasped, and fled from the cell in terror.

29

Uttermost West

I hardly noticed the mild spring evening as I rushed to the oratory where the rest of the brothers were chanting their prayers, but I saw their disapproving glances as I broke in, wildly calling for help.

Ciaran stepped to my side. 'What ails thee? Hast thou fallen sick?'

Although I knew I was babbling foolishly, I could not stop myself. 'God has cursed him and driven him out of every home he ever had for years upon years. Never forgiving or merciful. And it is he. He says he is the one who killed his brother and…'

'Quiet!' Brecan held up his hand sternly. He had grown up under Abbot Enda's stern rule and his word always settled our disputes.

'The old pilgrim has told me his story…' I began.

'So he has confessed to thee?'

'I think he meant to, yes.'

'Then the matter must remain thy secret. Didst thou absolve him?'

I shook my head.

'Did he not repent of his sins?' Brecan's tone grew

sterner. 'Use thy discernment, my brother. Surely he was not just boasting of wrongdoing?'

I tried to control my anxiety. 'Brother Brecan, I think he hates the Lord God and...and there is more besides.'

Brecan laid a finger to his lips. 'Count it an honour that he has entrusted himself to thee. If thou art still troubled, then bring thy worries to our Lord in thy private prayers.' I nodded unhappily. 'The pilgrim came to us seeking refuge,' Brecan turned to include the rest of the brothers in his words, 'and we must welcome him whatever he did in the past.'

I knotted my hands in desperation. 'He wants to speak to someone else. He was calling for a man called Patricius, but I know no one of that name.'

'Very well,' Brecan said patiently. 'Take me to him.'

When we entered the pilgrim's cell, I looked anxiously at the bed, but the old man did not stir until Brecan was seated on the wooden stool which I carried for him.

Suddenly the dark eyes opened. 'Thou art not Patricius. I do not wish to speak to any other.'

Brecan drew his brows together. 'I hear you are not at peace with our Lord, that you fear a curse.' I stepped back nervously, sure that the pilgrim would be angry at my betrayal.

He did not even glance at me as he replied. 'I am under a heavy doom, one that would drain the life blood from any ordinary man. I was doomed to wander without rest, and now I am too old, too old. I have suffered too long to find healing.'

'You are not too old to repent of your sins and be received as God's beloved child.'

The pilgrim's head sank back onto the pillow. 'The

blood I shed is still crying out for vengeance. It is too late for me.'

Recalling the close of his story, I dared to interrupt the conversation. 'But he has repented, Brother. He told me so. That is, he told another who also heard his confession once.'

Although the pilgrim made no response, Brecan's face creased into a smile. 'Then it is well. I can absolve him.' Getting to his feet, he made the sign of the cross above the bed and spoke the words of absolution. I watched the pilgrim for a trace of emotion.

'You are forgiven, my Father,' I said timidly. 'All your sins have been taken away.'

His reply crushed me. 'Everything taken away, my son? Even all my sins? Then I am truly nothing, a broken shell, worthless.' Outside the wind had risen a little and the dust on the cell floor stirred. 'I heard a voice calling me, but when I tried to follow, I found nothing. Now my hands are empty.'

'Every one of us has to strive after holiness and ask the Lord God to fill our emptiness with His presence.' Brecan stood up briskly. 'Now you should receive the sacrament as a sign of your absolution and reconciliation with God.'

'Dost thou forget?' the pilgrim said in a low voice. 'I am under a curse.'

Brecan looked down at him benevolently. 'The blood of Christ will deliver you from any curse and shield you in the days to come.'

The pilgrim's mouth spasmed with what I suddenly realised was horror. *It is the blood,* I told myself, *just as in his story. He cannot bear the blood.*

'Christ?' He spoke the word as if it held no meaning at all. 'What Christ? What blood?'

'Brother Brecan,' I said earnestly, 'believe him. I do not think he knows the full truth.'

Brecan drew breath, checked whatever he had been about to say and was silent for a long, thoughtful moment. Then he quietly told me to bring the holy oil and the reserved sacrament from the oratory. I went to do as he ordered, swallowing my questions.

On my way there, I met Ciaran who, when he heard my errand, said he would accompany me. As we left the chapel, reverently carrying the precious glass paten and chalice, I felt that we should linger outside a while, giving Brecan time to speak to the pilgrim. The sun had sunk below the horizon and the first stars were appearing in the night sky. Out over the dark sea I heard a gull cry and another answered further off.

'Is there really some deep mystery here?' Ciaran asked.

'I could not say,' I answered truthfully. After another moment or so, we set off back to the cell together. When we entered, Brecan was kneeling in prayer by the bed and the pilgrim lay with his hands folded over his chest. For an instant I wondered whether we had come too late, that maybe he was already dead. Then I saw his folded hands rising and falling with each slow breath. Hearing our footsteps, Brecan rose and beckoned for me to give him the oil. He opened the tiny flask and anointed the old man, repeating the customary prayer.

'I anoint thee with the oil of holiness in the name of God the Father, and of the Son, and of the Holy Ghost, so that thou shalt be saved in the name of the Holy Trinity.'

The pilgrim moved restlessly and said something I could not hear.

Brecan answered gently. 'Our Lord knows your heart, even if you have not the strength to declare it aloud.'

Nodding to Ciaran and I to join him, he said the collect for protection and deliverance from evil before taking the circle of unleavened bread and dipping it in the chalice.

Holding it to the old pilgrim's lips, he said, 'May the body with the blood of our Lord Jesu Christ be unto thee health to life eternal.' I felt strangely disappointed as I watched—but what had I expected? An old man taking his first and last communion. Should there have been light from heaven? The Holy Ghost in the form of a dove? I saw nothing except an aged, tired traveller sinking into what was surely his final rest. Maybe I felt around me a sense of peace, a sense of something accomplished. But I could not be sure.

Brecan, meanwhile, was giving him a blessing and saying a final prayer of thanksgiving.

'Come,' he said to us when he had finished, 'leave him to sleep.'

I followed him from the cell. 'Did he understand and believe? What didst thou say?'

Brecan smiled. 'Our Lord is merciful to those who repent and seek His face. I think all is well with our friend. Now, Brendan, it is time for thee to return to thy usual duties.' He forestalled my protest. 'Ciaran will take care of our pilgrim. You need rest as well.'

As I returned to my own cell, I realised how tired I was after my vigil. I mumbled my night prayers and dropped onto my hard bed, trying to make my last thoughts a prayer for the pilgrim.

When morning came, Ciaran spared time to reassure me that the old man was still sleeping peacefully, so my heart was easy when I went down to our community's fields to resume the work I had set aside a few days before. As I laboured, I enjoyed the clean air, the smell of the reshly-turned earth and the wind on my face. Apart from he customary times of prayer in the oratory, I worked vithout rest, and felt light-hearted in spite of my concern or the pilgrim. I promised myself that I would return to see him at the end of the day.

When the setting sun dazzled my eyes, I cleaned my hands on a hank of grass and began climbing back up the slope to where the cells stood like a group of huge beehives. Before I came to the encircling wall around our community, I walked a little way towards the cliffs and gazed out at the crimson sea, letting peace sink into my soul. *Our Lord is good,* I told myself. *Nothing can snatch us from His hand.*

When I turned my face to the cells again, I almost cried out. I thought I saw ghostly flames licking around the place where the pilgrim rested: red and gold lights flickering over the grey limestone. But when I blinked, they disappeared. Laughing at the trick played by the sunset, I started walking back.

Before I was halfway there, I saw Ciaran running towards me. His face told me the news he carried.

'The old man is dead.'

'When?'

'He drew his last breath just now. I saw thee by the cliff and was going to summon thee, but it was too late.'

At last, I thought. *He is at peace at last. Oh Lord God, may that be so.*

We buried him at noon the next day behind the oratory, chanting our prayers as rain poured down from a clouded sky. When the others had gone, I lingered, clutching a handful of soil and puzzling over something I had revealed to no one else.

While we were preparing the body for its final rest,

washing it and composing the limbs, I had noticed a change about the face. The features were inscrutable, expressionless, but it was something more tangible that concerned me.

Then as I stared at the withered right cheek, I understood what had changed. The scar was somehow smoothed away. Touching the cold flesh with my finger, I tried to trace the lines which had become familiar to me in the days and nights that I sat with the pilgrim, but I could not find them. None of the other brothers appeared to have seen anything different. I opened my mouth to tell Ciaran and stopped. Perhaps I was mistaken. Who could be sure about a face so aged, so shrunken? I kept my thoughts to myself.

And now I come to the end of my story, as the light grows too dim for me to see the words I trace so carefully. I have kept the pages hidden behind a loose stone in my cell, rolled in a leather pouch to protect them from damp and dirt.

My faith has been stripped bare by what the pilgrim told me. Before he came, I was a child with a child's blind faith, but now I must wrestle with the hard truths I have learned. Could it be that the story was true? I shall never know.

I wonder, though, whether a new path is unfolding at my own feet. Perhaps there is a pilgrim's way for me to take. I think it may lead me very far from the place I consider my home, but more than that I cannot say. May our Lord have mercy on us all. Amen.

The Lost And The Dreamer

by Naomi Starkey

Earth was diseased, burnt out. Two colony ships escaped. One was lost...

The settlement that grows from the surviving ship is in despair and disarray: families and civilisation break down as the colonists, repeating the mistakes of their forebears, ravage the new world of Osiris and fell the forests.

Four wanderers flee the riots and looting, their hearts fired with the dream of a better world. While Anno struggles on, impatient for freedom, Minna turns to dreams of a Prince with golden eyes who will come to her rescue. As they struggle over the pitiless mountains, facing betrayal and bloodshed, few signs of hope remain. Is there truly a Prince? Will he come?

'Enjoyable reading—a vivid tapestry.'

—**Fay Sampson**

Gospel End

by Rob Frost

When Geoff Notes, a young Methodist minister, is assigned the Yorkshire village of Gospel End for his first appointment, his heart sinks: to a boy from the London suburbs, Yorkshire seems the edge of the earth.

He and his publisher wife Sarah are horrified by what they find: a chapel bound by tradition, riddled with dry rot, locked in permanent opposition to the pub across the street.

Ignorant of local custom, Geoff shocks his flock by dropping in for a drink: a fine darts player, he soon makes many friends but alienates his congregation. Then the chapel collapses...

'A heart-moving story...God speaks in this book. He is using Rob Frost as he has used prophets through the ages.'

—VISCOUNT TONYPANDY

'Rob Frost's inimitably lively style....illustrates what can happen when a group of local Christians takes seriously the challenge of living and witnessing as the Body of Christ. I hope it will be widely read.'

—THE REVD DONALD ENGLISH

Minstrel
Published by Kingsway

The Final Boundary

by Adrian Plass

Life is a rich tapestry of emotions, memories and experience. Adrian Plass is one of the few Christian writers today who reflect that richness, wielding a pen at one moment like an artist's paintbrush, and at the next like a surgeon's knife.

To read these stories is to discover that a parable can 'entertain at the front door while the truth slips in through a side window'...the truth about ourselves, the games we sometimes play and the love we are all searching for.

ADRIAN PLASS, popular writer and broadcaster, has lifted the spirits of hundreds of thousands of readers with his *Sacred Diary* Series. Also in Minstrel paperback from Adrian: *Clearing Away the Rubbish* (Plus cassette).

Minstrel
Published by Kingsway